Widower [illegible]

Christmas, no[illegible]

Jordan fakes it, slapping on his best Christmas Cheer persona in the hopes of making it special for his son. Each year it gets a little bit easier. Who knows...maybe one year the holidays will be merry and bright.

When an unexpected blizzard comes to town, Alger and Jordan end up trapped together and learn that there really is magic in Christmas snow.

The Omega's Krampus Christmas is a super sweet with knotty heat MM Mpreg Holiday retelling of the fairy tale Beauty and the Beast featuring an alpha who accidentally pissed off the wrong elf, an omega who sees the heart within, more Christmas cookies than anyone should eat in a lifetime, a magical sleigh ride that leaves more than just Santa's bag being filled, the cutest cat ever...as in ever, Christmas wish lists a mile long, a Christmas miracle or two, including an adorable baby on the way. If you enjoy true love, fated mates, a little bit of whimsy, and your mpreg with heart, download The Omega's Krampus Christmas today.

The Omega's Krampus Christmas

Digital ISBN: 978-1-68361-598-9
Paperback ISBN: 978-1-68361-599-6
Hardback ISBN: 978-1-68361-616-0

The Omega's Krampus Christmas

by

Lorelei M. Hart

Prologue

Alger

Once Upon a Time

Teaching school paid next to nothing, but I had cheap lodgings and some of the families made me meals from time to time, which helped keep body and soul together. Some did not consider teaching a man's job, one that could support a family, but at least for the time being, my pleasure in helping to form young minds superseded any other factors.

Especially at the holiday season. On the last day of school before the Christmas vacation break, we suspended regular classes to bring all the classes together in the decorated auditorium for a holiday recital and festivities before sending the children to their frolics until the New Year.

This year, our class would be singing a selection of Christmas carols and I, dressed in the red suit of Saint Nick popularized by Clement Moore's *'Twas the Night Before Christmas* or *A Visit from Saint Nicholas* would appropriately read that story to close the event. As I prepared for my reading, a little sadness tugged at my heart. It was easy to pretend I had enough time with these children during class terms, but on holidays, when they were with their real families, the loneliness seeped in. Maybe I should have aspired to another career.

Sitting in the armchair placed at the front of the stage, with my students seated on the floor around me, my heart warmed. Sometimes the poverty many of them lived in daunted their spirits, but now smiles of pride at their performance lifted the corners of their lips. They'd indeed done well, and Santa Claus might have taken notice from his North Pole residence. I cleared my throat, bemused at my suspension of logic. Christmastime always made me sentimental, reminded me of my parents and brother, grandparents, all those who'd already departed this realm. They would celebrate the birth of the Christ Child with the angels in heaven, while I sat in my rented room eating whatever someone thought to bring me from their holiday table.

Even my landlady, who often included me in her holidays, would be away. I'd put her on the train myself, this morning, laden with presents and baked goods she'd prepared. I didn't resent her good fortune this year. Her married daughter had remembered she had a mother for the first time since my arrival and invited her for the festive season. Mrs. Dougherty's excitement had been contagious, buoying my spirits as I waved until the train disappeared down the tracks.

Such a good soul, she deserved happiness.

A tug on my trousers reminded me of where I was, and I began the poem. I recited more than read the beloved verses, putting as much heart into them as possible. My gift to the children whose faces I gazed into every school day, who learned their letters and numbers at my tutelage.

I taught the youngest of them, tasked with giving them a love of learning as much as any specific knowledge. If they had that love, they would do well going forward.

Finishing the reading, I closed the large book on my lap and chuckled as I thought Saint Nicholas might have before going up the chimney after laying out the gifts for the children of the house in the story.

Silence for a moment had me worried I'd not done justice to the tale, but then appreciative applause reassured me. The book was one my mother read the same story to me from, precious in its faded covers and holding just as much magic now as then. After I finished, the headmaster stood from his seat at the back of the stage and made a short speech. The same speech, word for word, as last year and the year before. But it suited the occasion and sent everyone off with a smile and a wave.

A few other teachers and I supervised some of the older boys putting the auditorium to rights before closing the school for two weeks. When we were done, and all the handmade decorations removed, it looked so dull. But clean and ready for the events of a new term.

As we were leaving, I spotted a bit of litter near the stage, so I bid the others goodbye, said I would lock the doors as I went, and crossed the room to pick it up. Alone, I looked around again. Just an hour or so ago, it had been filled with singing and laughter and bright colors both in the decorations and the students' and their families' holiday best attire.

Now, there was just me, in my brown jacket and trousers, not one sprig of greenery or red ribbon in sight. And since we'd turned down the furnace, the warm air in the room was being replaced by a distinct chill.

Time to go home.

I was about to leave the building when I saw a small boy sitting on a chair by the door, kicking his feet and staring at the floor. Little Timothy from my class. All by himself. I approached him and took the seat beside his.

"Timothy, did your fathers leave without you?" All the families were invited to the holiday recital, filling the auditorium with their appreciation for their children's performances.

"No, Mr. Bobell." His legs slowed their kicking but did not stop. Nor did he look up from his focus on the black-and-white tiles.

Oh. "They were unable to attend today, then." He looked so sad.

"They never come. Like they didn't come on Meet the Teacher night. Or our spelling bee or...or anything. Sir."

I didn't always get to speak to every parent when they came. Some were shy or just never made it to the front of the room for one reason or another. But from the children's reports, nearly all their parents or guardians attended when we invited them. Making the invitations was always a fun and popular activity for our art class the week before, and I had some very talented artists in my room this year. Timothy was one of the best. "Sometimes parents are very busy with their responsibilities and cannot take time to enjoy themselves. It's a shame. But we must try to understand."

He did lift his eyes to mine at that point, and they held all the pain and disappointment no child should have to experience.

"I have to lock up now, Timothy. Can you see yourself home?" Some did, and some others had a parent or older sibling to walk them.

"Yes, sir. I always go home alone."

Alone. I had a feeling he often arrived into an empty house. His worn shoes and everyday clothes had stood in stark contrast to most of the other children's holiday outfits, but poor didn't mean abused or neglected, and not all had new clothes. But his sad loneliness said it all. How had I not realized just how bad things were? Maybe because we were not allowed to interfere without students' outside of school, and parents had absolute authority there. Knowing they had it rough made it even harder to do my job and treat all the children equally.

Still.

Timothy stood and started for the door, but on a whim, I stopped him with a question. "Timothy, what is your wish this Christmas?" If it was within my power to grant it for him, I would, even if it meant I skipped a meal or two.

"A cookie," he replied. "Like my grandma used to make before she died."

My heart squeezed so hard, I gasped for a moment before recovering my breath. My mind worked furiously. Where had I seen cookies? A big cookie on a plate! "Timothy, do not leave. I will be right back."

I dashed down the hall to Mr. Samberg's class where, on his desk, sat a plate with a large, perfect, dark-brown molasses cookie. A single delight that might bring a smile to a young man's face. Mr. Samberg was gone already, and by the time we returned from our holiday, it would be gone anyway, food for a stray mouse.

Timothy was still there when I returned, and I gave him the cookie, thrilled to see the sadness retreat from his expression while he studied the marvel in his hands. "This is all for me? This whole cookie?"

"Merry Christmas, Timothy." I held the door open, turned off the lights, and followed him outside. "Be a good boy, and I'll see you after New Year's." I locked the door and by the time I turned to leave, the little boy was nowhere in sight. I wished I had so much more to give to this child and to the others who might have less-than happy Christmases for different reasons this year.

Like me, many had lost relatives in the Spanish Flu epidemic a few years before, others had folks who were out of work or had debt that made it impossible to buy things for a festive meal or gifts.

Saddened by the thoughts that not all the children I taught would have what all children should have for Christmas, I trudged away from the school building.

"Hey, you. I have a bone to pick with you, Mr. Teacher."

That couldn't be...but it was. An elf.

Chapter One

Jordan

Modern Day

"Daddy, are you going to make one of those sandwiches with everything from last night's dinner on it?" Thea looked up at me, and I couldn't quite discern whether she hoped for a yes or for a no response.

I personally loved *The Day After*, as my late mate used to call it. And maybe I loved that it was his thing and a way to remember him more than loving soggy bread with too much piled on. I tried not to think too hard on it. Thanksgiving had been the kickoff to the holiday season, and wallowing in my losses wasn't going to do either of us any good.

Thea deserved better.

"We ate Thanksgiving dinner at a restaurant," I reminded her. "I don't really have enough leftovers to make sandwiches." It has been our first year not traveling to a random family member's house since my mate died.

I had a suspicion the invites were to help keep me from suffering too much this time of year. After five holiday seasons, they'd likely deemed it enough time since Theo had passed to not need the hand-holding. And they were right. I didn't.

The phone went both ways. I could've invited them, too. Thought about it a couple of times, even. But it felt like this year we needed to be here. And just us.

"That's okay, Daddy. Maybe we can get one at the diner later?" Meaning, it wasn't really that okay. Poor kiddo. She'd been a toddler when her father passed, but Theo still lived in her heart.

My mother insisted she couldn't possibly remember Theo and that it was my fault she still remembered him, but she did remember him. And fuck that noise. Even if it was my memories being given to Thea, she deserved them. Every child deserves to know their father and, if the only way for that to happen was memories, then so be it.

"That sounds like a great idea. It's Black Friday, you know. We could even stop at the toy store, maybe."

"Black because it's the day Dad died?" she asked. And it wasn't really, not date wise, but it was the day after Thanksgiving that the hydraulic lift at work malfunctioned and our lives were changed forever.

"No, sweet girl, because it's when the stores make all the money. Red is when they lose money." It wasn't the best economics explanation ever, but given she was seven, it was probably enough.

"That makes more sense," she said after a long pause. "Can we stop at the pet store and look at the adoption dogs? Cookie needs a friend." Our cat Cookie did love dogs, but I wasn't sure she had an opinion on getting one or not.

We'd been heading to the adoption days pretty regularly since they started the program. Our closest shelter was a good hour away, and they paired up with the pet store to have adoption days for people to meet available dogs and cats. We'd been looking for a while, but we hadn't met our dog yet. The time we thought we had, the papers stated clearly they were not cat friendly.

"Absolutely."

She gave me a ginormous hug. "Let's go now!"

"Or... you could change out of your pajamas first."

Giggles erupted from her, and I couldn't help but join in.

"I forgot about that." She took off like a shot, thumping up the stairs toward her bedroom. For a tiny little thing, she sounded like Bigfoot heading up there.

"I'm getting the mail," I called up.

"I'll hurry," she yelled back down.

I slipped on my boots and headed out into the cold air and down to the end of the driveway where the mailbox lived. Sure enough, it was full. It was that time of year when catalogs and fliers were aplenty.

By the time I got back inside, the chill was starting to set in. I'd been living on the side of this mountain for five years and still wasn't used to the windchill it brought. Of course, I could've put on a coat, but who does that to get the mail?

"Is it here?" Thea ran down in her mismatched clothing, at least a dozen barrettes in her hair, and her doll Trudy in hand. She was ready to go.

"Is what here?" I looked through the mail, and, when I found the doll catalogue, I knew she was talking about. I held it up. "This?"

She squeed and raced to grab it. "Stacey at school said there is a new girl this year, and she has a pet dog."

"Is the new girl an old-fashioned one or a modern one?" I tried to keep up on all the doll gossip, but it was tough. There was always something happening in the doll world.

"She's from New Zealand and from now, I think. Stacey didn't say. She got her book on Monday!"

"Well, you have yours now. Do you want to read it in the car, or should we wait to go?" I didn't mind which we did. Today was about father-daughter time, not accomplishing tasks.

"I want to bring it. Is it cold?"

"Very. You'll need your warm coat."

"I gotta get Trudy her coat and say goodbye to Cookie." She ran back up the stairs, and I brought the mail to the kitchen table to deal with later.

I flipped through the fliers, hoping to find one for the pet store. If we did find a dog, we were going to hemorrhage money there getting food and a bed and all that fun stuff. There wasn't one, but there was a card addressed not to me but to Theo.

I didn't need to look and see who it was from. It was the same scammy insurance company who sent it every year. It didn't matter how many times I told them he was gone, they still sent it. You'd have thought I'd be used to it by now, but I wasn't. Every year, it hit me like a brick. Theo had never even lived here, but yet there he was on the list.

"Ready, Daddy!" Thea called from the next room.

I ripped the card in half and threw it in the trash. At least this year it didn't make me cry. It was time to move on and maybe, just maybe it was a sign I was ready.

"Let's go." I grabbed my keys, and we headed down the mountain to the small city closest to us.

The diner was packed with a line around the building, and we ended up grabbing fast-food burgers instead. There was something freeing about that. Like breaking that tradition was more than just eating the *wrong* lunch.

"Toy store?" I asked.

"Pet store," she insisted.

"If we find a dog, we won't be able to go to the toy store afterward," I explained.

"Daddy, I think a dog will help me not be sad about that."

"Pretty sure that's right."

The pet store was significantly less crowded than anyplace we had passed, which I appreciated. I held the door open for Thea and Trudy, the sound of Christmas music greeting us. And the music wasn't the only thing Christmas. The place was completely decked out.

"The adoptable pets are gone?" Thea looked to where they had been last month when they had an event and, sure enough, it was filled with Black Friday specials and not pets.

"We moved them to the back." A woman stepped over to us. "Are you here to adopt a dog or cat today?"

"Don't know," Thea said. "It depends on if the right dog for us is here today." It had taken a lot of work for me to get her to the point where she was no longer just wanting *a dog* but *the right dog*. She was growing up so fast.

"I hope the right one is here for you today. The elves brought them yesterday, so who knows." She waved us to follow her.

"If elves brought them, I don't want them," Thea announced firmly. "Elves can be mean."

The woman turned around and looked at me, her eyes pleading for help on what she should say or do next.

"Your father was scared of elves, not Santa's helpers, and I'm sure that's what these are," I informed my daughter.

Thankfully, she accepted that answer without hesitation. Probably because we reached the pet adoption area, where wiggly pups frolicked in their fenced area. "There are six this time." Thea grabbed my hand. "That's the most they have ever had!"

Which made me sad. I longed for the day when they didn't have any because all the dogs were happy in their forever homes. Not that that was a realistic goal.

"Two of them are brother and sister." The woman brought us to the end kennels. "This is Noel and Noelle. They are almost a year old."

In the kennel were the most adorable dogs. Had I not known they were almost full grown, I'd have assumed they were puppies. Definitely mixed breed with some corgi in the blend. It was difficult to not fall immediately in love with them.

"Their owner had to move into an assisted-living facility. They were well loved, but it just...they need to be adopted together. The other four are fine for solo adoptions. I just didn't want you to get your hopes set on one of these and be disappointed."

"Daddy, I think they were sent to us by Father, to make our Christmas happy. His favorite song was 'The First Noel'" she reminded me.

"Let's have a meet and greet to be sure."

And that was how Noel and Noelle became part of our family.

Chapter Two

Alger

I had no real job for 364 days of the year, 365 in Leap Years. My elfin encounter had ended with me finding myself at the North Pole where I lived in a small house at the very edge of the big man's compound. I wasn't the first to hold the position and title of Krampus, but since almost no one would even acknowledge my presence, and the one who did hadn't known my predecessor well, all I knew was that he either loved or hated sardines. Because the one real cupboard mounted on the kitchen area wall was packed to the top with cans of the slimy fishies, some of which looked old enough to have been canned before canning was a thing.

They did work well for ice fishing, as bait. I'd learned over the years to enjoy the fish available in the lakes and salt water nearby like arctic char, rainbow trout, salmon and, my favorite, arctic grayling. I'd never liked fish before the change, but since I wasn't into hunting, and those who did would never consider sharing it with Krampus, fish was the only fresh protein available to me, and I'd become a pretty good seafood chef.

So the seasons rolled around, marked only by the amount of sunlight brightening the snow. And as that lessened each year, as December arrived, so did showtime. December 5th...the day I left the North Pole to frighten the misbehaving children into behaving better. I didn't like it. I hated it. Having a monster like me loom over your bed and recite your "crimes" was an old-fashioned concept I had no interest in participating in. Yet, as the monster, cursed to be Krampus, my agreement was not required. I was compelled.

And I tried...I forced the limits of my compulsion, trying to explain to the children how their lying to their mom or stealing their brother's Pop Tarts...cheating on a spelling test—how did that even work?—would set them up for future failures. But even my softest, kindest voice could not pierce the horror of my face. My horns. My fangs. I was cursed to terrify children one day a year and regret it all the rest.

I tried not to go. I tried to hide my face. I considered ending my life, but, as the one person here at the North Pole who actually talked to me pointed out one day, Krampus could not die. I would remain cursed until I found true love.

“How is that possible?” I set down my empty cocoa cup with a klunk. I preferred tea but cocoa was always in stock here, tea not so much. And forget coffee. Santa said it made the elves edgy. “Where am I supposed to meet this true love?”

Ernie, the elf who’d changed me, refilled his mug from the pot, added a big dollop of whipped cream, and held out the plate of cookies he’d brought with him for our get-together. “Chocolate chip?”

“Why is it you’re all about sharing cookies with me now?” I accepted one, having learned long ago that it wouldn’t result in any further cursing. “You sure acted differently once that I recall.” When he first started coming over, I had not confronted him about such things, but after a century of twice-a-week afternoon cocoa breaks together, I wasn’t worried. He was the only person in this whole benighted town who acknowledged my existence...the very one who put me in this position. Even when I took fish to the trading post to exchange for supplies, the transaction took place in uncomfortable almost silence. “Six arctic char, one bag sugar, one bag flour, cocoa, no tea. One case sardines." Even a full cupboard of sardines couldn't last forever. And I'd tried other bait but never caught a single arctic grayling with anything else.

I never traded grayling. They were hard to come by, and those who ignored me didn't deserve them.

"You ate my cookie. And you didn't even ask first."

"You know that's not what happened."

He dunked a cookie in his cocoa. "I used dark chocolate chips and pecans in this batch. What do you think?"

"I think a guy who bakes treats this good shouldn't have changed a man into Krampus for giving a single molasses cookie to a little boy."

He narrowed his eyes. "A single very large cookie. I had been looking forward to it all afternoon, waiting for everyone to leave. Then, just when it's time, bam! It's snitched."

We'd had this conversation for about eighty years. I shouldn't even bring it up. Still...like scaring the kids, I couldn't seem to stop myself. "Edwin, change me back."

"What's done can't be undone." He held up a cookie, perfectly browned at the edges, a little soft in the middle. "Like this cookie. I put nuts in it. Maybe you'd prefer not to have nuts in your snacks." He arched a brow, waiting for me to answer. You get to know a guy after a while, what his expressions and actions mean. When there's no one else, you make a study of him.

"I like nuts just fine. As you know. Your nut brittle dipped in gold leaf is a masterpiece." I settled back in my seat, unwilling to have more cocoa and yearning for coffee. I'd been trying to figure out how to get some for the longest time but never had any extra moments when I was on my journey. Santa's coffee rule sucked eggs. Also, rumor had it that he wasn't above an occasional espresso himself on his travels.

"Anyway, let's say, for spits and giggles"—*elves don't cuss. I don't think they can*—"that you hated nuts. I might wish I had a way to get them out of the cookies, but I wouldn't, would I?" Another arched brow. We were really getting in a rut.

"No, you wouldn't."

"What's done cannot be undone. So it is written, so it must be."

I didn't say amen. I had once, and then had to explain why I considered his pronouncement worthy of that add-on. He didn't get it. I didn't repeat it.

"Edwin...would you like to come over tomorrow for dinner?" He wasn't always the best company, but he was my only company.

"Grayling?" He smacked his lips.

"As long as you don't tell anyone."

"It's our secret."

And without him, I'd be so lonely, I wouldn't be able to go on. It was a conundrum.

As we sat there in the little house, the flames crackling in the fire, I wondered how long I'd be here, how many centuries. Watching the wheel of the year turn. Eating cookies and fish.

That little boy, the one I gave the cookie to, how had his life turned out? I'd thought of him often but never had reason to visit him, so he must have been a good child. All the children in my class would be grown up and old and gone by now. Lives spent, married, raised families of their own. Had jobs and illnesses, happiness and tragedy. I prayed often that they had rewarding existences.

While I sat here in this little house, despised by those whose lives were dedicated to delighting children. Mine was dedicated to children but to punishing them. Frightening them. Making them cry. My throat tightened, vision misted. I was a poor example of a terrifying beast. My time was coming soon, the sun only pushing the shadows back for a short time each day. Dread grew. Faces of little children who I'd frightened swam in front of my eyes. The reasons for their seeing me seemed so minor in the scheme of things. All children made mistakes or were mischievous. Did they deserve a visit from me?

I had no mirror in the house. I'd caught a glimpse of myself here and there, in the homes of those I visited, enough to know how ugly I was. Not that I'd ever considered myself dapper or a dandy...or handsome, but I'd gotten my share of smiles from the single ladies.

"Edwin, do you have any suggestions on how I might find this true love? Because everyone here hates me."

"I don't hate you." His voice was soft. "And neither do the others. You have a very different mission from theirs. They picture all the children they serve as little angels. You are a reminder that they are human and maybe will be selfish with the game or rough with the doll they make. It's easier to pretend you don't exist."

"In a way that's worse than hatred." We sat again for a while, watching the fire, while outside darkness gathered and the wind came up, whooshing around the corners of the little house.

Finally, Edwin stirred. "I need to go, but thank you for the cocoa."

I stood and got his coat. "Thank you for the company."

He put his arms into the sleeves and fastened the toggles. "One day, you may thank me for what I did all those years ago."

"I doubt it." I shook my head sadly. "Goodbye."

Chapter Three

Jordan

"I don't know, you two," I looked down at the two dogs nestled together on the couch beside me. "I think we might be getting more snow than the weather report said."

The snow was coming down at a good clip from what I could tell through our picture window. It was a gorgeous sight. I'd left the porch light on, grabbed a mug of cocoa, and joined our two new fur babies on the couch to watch the snow fall.

It was something I used to do with my grandfather when I'd stay over, and it brought me back to a carefree time in my life. A time when snow falling meant Santa was coming soon. A time when Christmas magic was real.

We sat there, the three of us, for a long time, the dogs first starting to doze and me finally following. I'd probably have stayed there all night if I hadn't been awoken by the cold. It was freezing.

I opened my eyes to find the room dark, not even the light from the porch shining through the window.

"Great," I grumbled. "The power is out. Again."

It wasn't unheard of to lose power in a storm up here. It happened often enough that I'd had a generator installed a couple of winters back. It was enough to keep most things going. But, of course, it was broken, the part taking a bazillion years to come in. At least the repair tech had let us borrow a small one in case of emergencies. It wasn't enough to do everything, but it kept the refrigerator and well pump going as well as the light in Thea's room. Somehow her light was on the same circuit as the fridge, and I wasn't sad about it.

I went over to the quilt rack and grabbed a few. They were hand quilted by my father, and I usually only used them as decoration, but until the house was warm again, they were going on Thea's bed.

Holding them close to both heat them up and keep me warm, I tiptoed up the stairs, the dogs not moving from their spot on the couch. They were sound asleep, a pile of fur. They'd make the world's worst watchdogs, but they were the perfect addition to our home.

I crept into Thea's room, my phone as a flashlight. She was sound asleep on her side, Trudy beside her on her own pillow and a stuffed dog held tightly in Thea's arms. I covered her up and left the door open to allow the heat to come in. As soon as I got the woodstove started.

"Sleep well, sweet girl," I whispered and Cookie started to purr…loudly. I hadn't even seen her, but she was under the covers somewhere. "Be a good kitty and keep our girl warm."

After a quick trip through the upstairs opening doors later, I headed out to get the generator running. I'd kept it in the back shed, thinking we wouldn't need it. It was still so early in the season after all. But I should've known better.

"Why did I have to be right?" I stepped onto the porch to see far more snow than I wanted to see and, worse, it was still coming down. I trudged out to the shed and grabbed the generator and, just as my fingers and toes had started to lose feeling, I got it set up and running.

"Time for the woodstove."

In hindsight, starting the fire first would've been a better idea. Coming in from the cold was much easier when the house was nice and toasty. I tried to start the fire, but my fingers weren't cooperating. They were just too cold.

Noel came over and bopped me with his nose.

"Hey, what's got you up? You're supposed to be sleeping and staying warm with your sister."

He started to pet himself with my hand. Poor guy just wanted attention.

"Did you think I left you?" I cooperated. No dog should have to pet themselves. They were put on this earth to be spoiled. "I promise you, I didn't. It's scary though, isn't it?"

He leaned his full weight against me, soaking in my affection.

"Scary when your people are suddenly gone. They are supposed to be there for you every day. Only that's not how it always works out."

Noelle nudged me from behind.

"I didn't hear you get up, girl."

She was just as wanting of affection as her brother.

"We are glad you're here."

She licked my nose, and I wiped away the moisture.

"Look at that, you two." I wiggled my fingers. "You warmed me up enough to get this fire going."

Or so I thought. The fire didn't want to light. I tried my kindling and newspaper, and even a fireplace candle I'd been gifted last Christmas. None of them worked.

"I'm going to turn the water on to stop the pipes from freezing. You two go sleep well and stay warm."

If I couldn't get the blasted thing started by morning, I was going to need to dig us out of here and head into town. That sounded easy and like a great plan and it would be if the snow wasn't still falling, the plow came up this way swiftly, and my tires had chains.

There was no reason for the woodstove to be so problematic. None. If I hadn't known better, I'd have agreed with Theo when anything didn't go his way. *Darn Elves*. Maybe that was it. Maybe an elf was blowing it out as I lit it. It was as good of an excuse as any.

I turned on the kitchen and bathroom sinks, letting the water dribble down. As long as it was flowing, the pipes should be fine. At least as long as the temperature didn't drop...which it would once the snow stopped.

Back downstairs, I went back to work, and this time the fire started with ease.

Meow.

"Cookie, did you get cold?" That was strange. She usually stayed in Thea's room until morning. Maybe the cold had gotten to her. "Let's bring Thea another blanket while this place warms up."

Chapter Four

Alger

And lights, camera...action!

But where in the name of Christmas was I?

Every year, the power of whatever lay behind the curse that kept me in this terrifying form sent me to the center of a populated area where I'd be able to do my job aka scare some children into being good.

Or at least better.

I hated this day, hated showing my frightening face to kids who really weren't that bad at all in my opinion. Sometimes, I wondered if my appearance might not scare them straight but have the opposite effect. When I was a child, I would have been terrified and maybe run right off a cliff or something to get away. Oh, I knew the rules, and without this day, I'd have been completely without any use to anyone, just an appalling creature living on the outskirts of Santa's Village, but I prayed that the curse was only on me and not the children I visited.

Maybe this year was different. A snowy white landscape spread around me as far as the eye could see, and one thing about this form I was stuck with—it came with perfect vision. The few scattered trees and boulders were coated with the stuff, and the low-hanging clouds promised much more before the sky would clear again.

Hmm.

How was I supposed to do my job with nobody around?

"Mister?" The voice cut through my thoughts, accompanied by a tug on my sleeve. "Mister?"

I blinked, sure I was imagining things. The countryside around me had been empty; I'd swear to it, but when I tipped my face downward, sure enough, there was a little girl, about seven years old, looking back at me. She wore a long coat, too big for her as if it was someone else's. And slippers. They had to be soaked through, her feet chilled to the bone, but rather than seeming upset or sad, she studied me inquiringly.

"Mister, are you Santa's helper?"

A question I had literally never been asked. I mean—why would anyone? I didn't have white hair and a fluffy beard. I had long red hair that had a tendency to get stringy or tangle if I didn't keep it carefully combed. And cutting it did no good. Cut it, go to bed, wake up with it just as long as before I attempted the change. It was probably part of the persona like the huge ram-like horns curling out of the top of my head. Try to sleep with those, why don't you? For the first hundred years or so, I bumped them into the headboard so often, I'd finally just given up and dragged the mattress into the middle of the floor.

And my teeth! Santa Claus, in my experience, did not have a mouthful of sharp choppers that looked like they were made for slashing. No, while his teeth might be extraordinarily white and perfectly straight, they were, other than that, blunt and very human in appearance.

I self-consciously curled my claws into my palms. Like the hair, they were unchangeable—but not because they grew back. They were literally impossible to cut. Every part of me was designed to scare naughty children into behaving. Hell to scare—terrify, horrify, and panic them. I'd read my own reviews where I was called awful, grim, horrifying, ghastly, grim, and the stuff nightmares were made of.

Considering none of the reviews were written by a child who'd actually seen me, I thought they were presumptuous, but what they did helped bolster my reputation.

"Mister, are you?" The little girl shifted from foot to foot, woolen slippers probably doing nothing to prevent frostbite. "Are you Santa's helper?"

"In a way." Of course, I was. And his scapegoat, but no point in going into that with a child while the storm deepened into a blizzard. "What are you doing out here?"

"I need sticks to start a fire. I'm c-cold." She shivered. "I can't find the sticks because the snow is too deep."

Indeed, as we'd stood there, the snow had gotten so deep, I couldn't even see those slippers anymore. "Well, I have a bundle of sticks." They were for naughty kids—and I usually called them switches—but she was probably naughty in some way just to be out here. For one, that coat was not hers. It had to be borrowed or stolen from someone much larger. "But I don't think they're going to do us much good. Not in this storm."

She shivered harder. "But without a fire, we can't get warm. Aren't you cold, mister?"

"A little." Not strictly true. It was chilly, but compared to the average day the North Pole, this was mild. "How about if I take you home. Your dads must be worried about you."

She didn't reply, and I wondered why. I usually had all the information I needed about the kids I encountered but not this time. But as Krampus, my job was to scare, maybe even punish, but not to allow a child to die of the cold. What redemption lay in that?

She was still quiet, but the longer we stood here, the greater the danger to her. "Climb in my basket." I bent so she could get into the basket hung over my shoulder. "And we'll get you home to your family." Maybe once I resolved this situation, I would be able to get on with my work and get this worst day of the year over with. I wasn't sure she'd do it at first, but just before I was about to straighten up and try to think of another way, she seemed to decide and scrambled into the basket.

I stood. "There you go." She thought I was Santa's helper. Did she not see how horrifying I was? Her trust in even getting in the basket didn't make sense. And her dad needed to teach her to be more wary of strangers. Especially strangers with claws.

Chapter Five

Jordan

"Cookie, I'll go check on her." I petted the cat who then went to the back door where both the dogs now sat and stared. "I'm not letting you out. You'd hate it. There's a ton of snow."

I brushed my thighs off, grabbed the last quilt from the rack, and went upstairs. Finding her bed empty, I figured she had to be in the bathroom, so I laid the blanket on top of the others and waited for her. One minute ticked by and then another.

"Crap." I'd forgotten about the lights. Poor Thea was probably scared to leave the bathroom.

I headed to it to find it empty. Trying not to panic, I checked my room in case she had been scared. Nothing. Then I ran downstairs to the second bathroom. She wasn't there, either.

But now the dogs were scratching at the door. They'd never done this, but then again, we hadn't had them for long.

Something in my gut told me to open the door and, when I did, my heart stopped. Little footprints marked the snow outside. She'd left. I ran back inside, slipped on my boots, and reached for my coat. But the hook was empty. At least she was warm? I was grasping at anything that resulted in her being safe.

I couldn't lose her. I couldn't. She was all I had left in the world. I racked my brain trying to think of how long she might've been out there. What kind of a father lost their daughter in a snowstorm? I had one job. One. It was to keep her safe, and I failed.

"Thea!" I called over and over again, following the steps to the bottom. The snow was falling hard and the wind blowing intensely. I looked over my shoulder and couldn't see the house, but the dogs were at my heels. The snow was too deep for them, and I ordered them to go back. I couldn't keep them safe and find her. It was too much.

All of this was too much.

To my relief, they obeyed, taking shelter on the porch, which at least had a roof, as I trudged through the snow. Why had she left? If she'd gone out to play in the snow, she'd have taken her own coat and mittens. Something had her leaving in a hurry.

I walked and walked, calling out her name until I was hoarse and kept on calling.

A huge deep roar echoed through the air. We didn't live where there were huge game animals. Not even close. The largest were some small brown bears that didn't even come up to my height. Unless you included herbivores like the moose, and no herbivore made that sound.

I picked up my pace, running in the direction of the sound, my visibility obscured by swirling snow. I ran into a tree. It knocked me on my ass. I didn't have time for this. I needed to get to Thea and keep her safe.

Except it wasn't a tree.

"Daddy! I did it. I got sticks so we can get the fire going." Thea. Thea was here but not alone. I ran into someone. I felt it.

I struggled to my feet, wiping the snow from my face so I could see who'd saved her. Who I needed to thank for my baby's life, her safety. No one lived close enough to be out this far, so I couldn't imagine who it might be. We lived on the side of a freaking hill, for goodness sakes.

The moon hit just right and I saw him—them—it wasn't a person. It wasn't a deer. It was something from the page of horror books. No. Not a horror book. From the page of a Christmas book, one my grandmother had as a child. It scared me then, and it terrified me now. Not only was there a freaking real-life Krampus standing in front of me, not saying a word, but he was wearing his basket—the one he used to collect children who'd been naughty.

"No. You can't be real." It had to be a dream. This couldn't be real. It was just a nightmare, the kind that would prevent me from sleeping for the next ten thousand nights.

And Thea's head poked out of it just then. "Daddy, I met a friend."

I rushed to grab her from the Krampus and he didn't attempt to stop me. He didn't help me, either. He just stood there and watched me, as if fascinated.

"Give her back!" I was afraid to hit him, afraid it would make him disappear, or worse, hurt Thea in the process. Trying to get her was the best plan I could think of and it wasn't working.

"Daddy, this is Santa's helper. He has sticks for us and his basket is so warm. Can I stay here? He's taking me home." There was not an ounce of fear in her voice.

"He's not Santa's helper. Help me get you out."

"But he is. He is," she insisted. "Tell him, my friend. Tell him how you found me."

"You found me, little one." He chuckled. Chuckled. Wasn't he supposed to be a fear-invoking, child-snatching monster. “And yes, I help Santa and the elves. My job isn’t as fun as making toys though.”

His voice was so reassuring. As if all the lore I heard was a lie. But how could it be? He had my daughter in a freaking basket.

“No. Don’t lie. You can’t be an elf’s helpers. They are bad. Elves are very very bad.” It was the first time I sensed fear from her. “Take it back.”

“Well, I have to agree with you. Elves are not the best. One day, ask me about a cookie.” One day. As if I was going to see him again. As if we were going to see him again. “But right now, let’s get you home. I don’t want to miss my way home, and you need to get out of those wet slippers.”

“Slippers,” I gasped. Of all the things to be freaking out about, that probably wasn’t it, but thinking of her feet turning black from the cold overtook the rest of it.

Or maybe it was because I didn’t feel that unsafe with the Krampus anymore. What was that about? Cold delirium? Was that even a thing?

“You won’t take her?”

“No. I promise not to take her. I don’t take children. That’s a myth.” He started walking towards the house. "I don't even like to scare them." He said the last part softer, or maybe the wind roared louder. But still...there was truth in his words.

"I'm not happy you left the house," I told Thea, holding her hand over the basket as he walked through the snow with ease, slowing down when it became more difficult for me.

"Here you are." He ducked down at the base of our steps, and I grabbed Thea, holding her tight and starting upward.

"You coming in for cocoa?" Thea asked him. "I won't offer you a cookie because it sounds like you hate them."

At the sound of Cookie's names, the dogs yipped. They wanted their cat back.

"I don't know if that's a good idea. I'm scarier in the light."

"Mister, you're Santa's helper. There's nothing scary about that. I'm cold. Come in."

"She's stubborn." I let out a sigh. "Might as well come inside."

And a huge part of me wanted him to. I refused to think too hard on that. For now, I needed to get my baby girl warm and probably ground her to her room for a few decades.

Chapter Six

Alger

I have one job. I work one day a year. And instead of doing my job, traveling from place to place and scaring naughty children straight, helping them to see the error of their ways, showing them the switches that my predecessors had done more than display, I had accepted an invitation for cocoa.

As to the switches, I had never used them in my tenure. Perhaps a Krampus was needed to help these little scamps change their naughty ways, but I would not be switching anybody. They could make me look like a monster, but I had my limits.

As I watched my new little friend and her dad mount the stairs, I almost turned and left. They couldn't really want me in their home. And even if the child did, her father thought I was an even worse monster than I was.

But the little girl waved at me over his shoulder. "Come on, mister. And bring the sticks."

The sticks. I rolled my eyes and followed them into their home. It was small but neat, and two dogs watched me from a corner, their gaze suspicious although they stopped short of barking. I wouldn't have blamed them if they did. Even a dog knows a monster when they see one.

"Thea, let's get you out of these wet things." The man sat her on a bench by the front door and stripped off the heavy oversized coat and the slippers. He examined her toes and fingers, her earlobes and nose for frostbite, then gave a nod of satisfaction. "All right. I don't see any damage, but you gave me the fright of my life."

Then he stood her up and turned her toward a staircase. "Now, you run up and change to your fuzzy Santa jammies and some warm socks while I make the cocoa, okay?"

Thea. My friend's name was Thea. When I was sent to particular children, I usually knew their name, but this was not a naughty one. Something must have gone on the fritz for me to even end up with her, but I was glad I had. If I hadn't...well, I didn't want to think about that.

It didn't take long for a child to get cold enough to just lie down and fall asleep. If that happened, her daddy wouldn't have been able to find her in time. My heart twisted at the thought as her little feet thudded up the stairs, bare but perfectly fine.

Nobody told me where to go or gave me any written assignments. As the dark side of Christmas magic, the Krampus appeared where he was supposed to. Usually.

"Do you take marshmallows?"

I startled at the question, my gaze shooting from the child disappearing down an upstairs hallway to the man who faced me with one brow arched. "Do I take them for what?" My face burned at my misunderstanding. "Sorry, you mean in hot chocolate."

"Yeah, what else could I have meant? I mean, I suppose we could make s'mores, but we were talking about cocoa."

"Right. Cocoa. Yes, that would be nice. I'm Jordan by the way. Do you go by Krampus?"

"Unfortunately, yes. And just so you don't think I'm deluded as well as ugly—" I held up a hand before he could respond. "Don't even try to deny it. But on the question of marshmallows, at the North Pole, they are sometimes used for currency. Homemade marshmallows are worth at least six scones or maybe four truffles."

He studied me a long time, holding a saucepan in one hand and a bag of marshmallows in the other before he burst into laughter. "You had me going for a minute there. Marshmallow currency. So what's a candy cane worth?"

"Virtually nothing. They sprout everywhere, like dandelions down here."

He shook his head and set the pan on top of the woodstove. "I'd like to see that one day."

"It's full of elves." I winked at him.

"No elves, Daddy!" Thea was already coming down the stairs sitting down, sliding on her pajama-clad bottom and sock feet. "Elves are bad."

She was looking at me, a scary monster who, even if she hadn't heard the stories about Krampus, should be enough to terrify any adult much less a child, and calling me Santa's helper. Elves, who could be pretty adorable when they wanted to, she feared. "Some are," I corrected her. "But they are also very busy up there, especially this time of year, getting all the toys ready for Christmas. So, visitors wouldn't be welcomed right now." Or pretty much ever.

"Come here, Thea." Jordan stood in front of a big chair set near the woodstove. "I want to get you all cozy while I make our cocoa. Maybe your new friend can tell you about marshmallows at the North Pole. They use them to buy things!"

"Only the homemade kind," I corrected. "Never the store-bought ones in a bag. They'd be worth less than candy canes."

Thea peered out of the nest of quilts her father had wrapped around her. "You can make marshmallows?"

"Well, I can't." I'd never even considered trying. "But I've traded some fish that I've caught in the lakes for them, and they are amazing."

"So who makes them?" Her eyes widened. "Elves?"

"Yep." I accepted a mug of cocoa with the aforementioned store marshmallows floating in it. "Elves. So you can see some of them are nicer than others."

"Because anyone who makes homemade marshmallows can't be all bad." Thea wrestled her arms free of her cocoon to accept her own cup, one with Santa's smiling face beaming out on the side.

Jordan set his cup on the small table in front of the sofa and sighed. "Okay, if we're all settled, why don't you two tell me what exactly happened out there in the wilderness before I found you." He gave us both a stern glance—one I didn't think I deserved, since all

I'd done was keep his child from freezing. Still...I couldn't hate that he was looking at me without fear or disgust. "And don't skip any details."

As we sipped the hot chocolate, with the dogs at our feet and a very sweet cat purring on my lap, we took turns filling the worried dad in on the occurrences once Thea came upon me in the storm. Listening to it now, relating it now, I was struck by just how close this family came to being destroyed. And judging by Jordan's pale cheeks, he knew it, too. How could he not?

"Daddy, can I have a cookie?" Thea's piping voice cut into the silence that had fallen with the realization on the part of the adults.

"Sure, of course." Jordan stood and scooped up his empty mug. He set it in the sink and picked up a cookie tin. Bringing it back with him, he opened it and stared inside. "What are these?"

"Cookies?" Thea asked hopefully. "Christmas cookies with sprinkles?"

When he continued to stare, I stood up and went to his side. "Oh, molasses cookies. I'll have one of those." They couldn't make me worse than Krampus, could they?

"I don't know that kind." But Thea was still ready to grab one when her father lowered the tin. She took a big bite. "These are yum! But they need sprinkles."

I bit into mine and sighed. "They really are good."

"I guess I bought the wrong kind at the bakery," Jordan mused. "I never even looked in the tin. But they do look elegant in an old-fashioned way. I wonder if they charged me enough."

"They often come with a high price."

Chapter Seven

Jordan

I have a feeling I know why Santa sent Krampus to us." I directed my firm words toward Thea. I was trying to do the gentle-parenting thing, but even as we sat her with our new...with Krampus, all that kept going through my head was wandering out on Christmas morning and finding her frozen little body in the snow. Had Krampus, a creature I hadn't ever truly believed in, not been there, I'd have lost everything tonight.

"Because you're lonely and need a new friend?" Thea was right. I was, and I did, but that had absolutely nothing to do with the issue at hand.

"No. Because what you did tonight was so naughty. Naughty enough a Krampus had to be sent here instead of Europe where they usually go." At least, I'd never heard of one being here. But then again, even if I had, I most likely wouldn't have believed it.

"I was trying to help you," she said sternly.

"But?" She knew where she turned wrong, and I expected her to admit to it.

"But I am not big. I'm small, and I need to ask a grown-up before going anywhere because the world isn't as safe as it could be and I won't do it again." She spoke more like a little robot than a child, and I instantly felt guilty for it.

Parenting was hard.

"It isn't safe, and you scared me so much." I opened my arms, and she came over and hugged me tight. "I love you, Thea, and I can't...please don't do that again."

"You're afraid I was going to be with Dad," she said, her voice cracking as if it all finally clicked.

"I was, sweet girl. I was."

"I miss him, too, but I won't go. I promise. I'll be safe." It was all I could do to hold back the tears at her words.

"I know you will." I kissed the top of her sweet head. "Now get some sleep. It's almost time to wake up."

"Night, Daddy." She kissed my cheek and then ran over to Krampus and gave him a huge hug.

"Thank you, Krampus. My daddy would've been so sad if you hadn't been there. I wish you could stay. Will you come back next year?" She was still holding onto him tightly, and he gently wrapped his arms around her after looking to me for approval.

“I don’t get to pick where I go, and it’s always to kids who are naughty. This year was a mistake, a mistake I’m very pleased occurred because it means you’re okay. But I don’t know if I can come back.” There was a longing in his voice.

No part of him seemed like the cruel beast of the stories. If anything, he was the opposite. Like the huge blue monster in the book Thea liked so much. It sucks to be born into a career the way he had. It wasn’t like he applied for the job or had an online recruiter seek him out. I hated it for him.

“Then I will write you letters. I can mail them to Santa and have him give them to you.” I wasn’t quite sure that would work. It wasn’t as if the post office had a way to get the letters to him. Or maybe they did. Everything I thought I knew was turned on its head tonight with meeting Krampus.

Maybe I was dreaming.

“I would like that, Thea.”

Two more hugs, and she went off to bed, the dogs following her up. Cookie? She stayed put. Either she was miffed at being disturbed mid-sleep, or she was as over the top in love with Krampus as she seemed. She sat in the chair behind him, purring and purring like a little motor.

Not one of us was scared of the beast. And that defied logic. I wouldn't say the dogs loved him. They didn't, but they didn't mind him there, either. The entire thing was...this had to be a dream—one of those nightmares you managed to turn around. That was the only logical conclusion.

"She's a really great kid." Krampus picked up his mug and drained it. "A really great kid. I hate that she acted so dangerously, but also—it was from such a giving place." He set his mug down.

"Her father died," I said, wanting him to understand. He didn't need to. Krampus was here for a night and then gone for...forever. But still, I wanted him to know how deeply tonight's events sliced through me. "An accident. This time of year. And I've never been so scared as tonight. I can't thank you enough. I wish you didn't have to go." And I meant it. Just the thought of him leaving already had me sad. It made no sense, but what of this did?

"I was worried when I saw her, too. I'm just grateful she wasn't scared of me. It could've been a very different outcome."

I'd not thought of that, and it sent a shiver through me. "She sees people for who they are. It's a gift of hers." One that had me trusting her instincts; whenever she disliked someone, I avoided them. Full stop.

"I'm not a person." He looked down, no longer meeting my eyes, and stood up. "I need to go before I miss my ride."

"Do you come on a sleigh?" His mode of transportation was not something I needed or was even sure I desired to know. It was the only question I could think up quickly, and I wanted him to stay if only for a few minutes.

"No. I don't really know how I get where I'm going."

Cookie put her front paws on his legs and meowed.

"She doesn't want you to go." *And I don't, either.*

"Sorry, pretty kitty. I don't get to decide these things. I'll put in a good word with Santa. Maybe he can get you a condo or something." He reached down and pet her goodbye.

"She used to have a cat condo. It broke, but she did love it." Again more talking to stall. What was wrong with me?

He started toward the door and, before I thought it through, I crossed over to him and gave him a hug. "There are not enough thanks for what you did today."

His arms slowly came around me and, just as he grazed my body with them, he snapped them back as if second-guessing his choice.

"I'm glad I was here."

And off he went into the snow and cold and out of my life.

Cookie mewed at the door, crying for him to come back.

"It won't work, Cookie." I bent down and scooped her up and into my arms. "I wish it would, but it won't. He doesn't belong here, even if it feels like he does."

I went back into the living room and sat in front of the woodstove, staring at the flames, listening to the crackling as the fire hit the sap, and thought about the irony that my next fire would be started with a switch, a Krampus's switch.

No, not a Krampus; Krampus.

Did he have another name? He had to have. There were more than one Krampus. Or at least I was pretty sure there was. The lore had bunches of them to collect all the evil little children. But they weren't evil children; they were mischievous. And he said that he didn't take children.

"If he comes back, Cookie, I can ask him all the things. Like if his name is George. I think it might be. He comes across like a George."

I sat there for a long while, thinking about everything he said, dissecting it, looking for hidden meanings.

Maybe I could write a letter to him, too. He was the first person to ever agree with my late mate that elves could be bad. Maybe there were other things he could tell me. Or maybe he could come over and eat lasagna, and we could try to make homemade marshmallows so he could buy things up north. Or maybe he could...

"You're being ridiculous." I chastised myself. "He's Krampus, and he doesn't belong in our world." Even if it felt like there was a hole there now that he had left.

Chapter Eight

Alger

I'd left a few of my switches for their fire. Not that it was allowed—at least I didn't think it was. They had only one use, and a use I'd never put them to. But as I trudged down the steps, I was afraid they might not have enough kindling, so I turned and climbed back up to leave all the rest.

It might be bad for me to show up at my next stop with no switches, but since they were only for show, why not let them serve a purpose? Let them burn up and never be used to hurt a child. In all my decades in this office, I'd never used them for anything at all. In fact, the basket of switches I left were the ones my predecessor had supplied. And it felt good to leave them behind. I'd probably have to make more. Maybe. Or I'd get back to find the cupboard in the corner refilled with a bunch more.

But these? These would help to keep a family I'd already grown fond of warm in the coldest of nights. Leaving again was even harder. This had been my first "normal" interaction with people in such a long time. At the North Pole, I was tolerated. Elves kept mostly to themselves, reported to Santa. They were glad to trade their goods for fish, but they didn't do it with great warmth. In fact, I'd have to call them jerky to me. As if I was a necessary evil.

I supposed I was.

Amazing that the one elf who spent any time with me at all was the one I should bear such resentment against. And I did, in the beginning, but over time, he'd become the closest thing I had to a friend.

I'd almost forgotten what it was like to sit down with actual humans and enjoy cocoa and conversation. To spend time with a child who wasn't frightened of me. The snow whirled around me, making it difficult to see where I was going. So cold. Not that I really suffered from the chill, but the warmth in front of Jordan and Thea's woodstove was more than just a difference in air temperature.

The warmth in their home had melted some of the ice that had formed around my heart. Not all of it, I'd spent too long building it up. But the outer edges, softening the sharp pain in my chest I'd almost forgotten was even there. Even the silly store-bought marshmallows—something the candy-making elves would have used for cannon fodder in the next snowball fight—tasted fluffy and smooth and special.

And the cocoa was so creamy and smooth. Without a single candy cane in it, the way it was always served up north. Even though Santa put at least one in every stocking, the wild-growing treats threatened to take over the place and had to be used any way possible.

The snow came up to my knees when I got to the bottom step and started out again. But I never had to walk very far, Christmas Magic carrying me from one place to the next. Worked every time. A fact I reminded myself of as the house with the little family disappeared into the blizzard behind me.

I lifted one foot after the other, moving forward and wondering when I'd be lifted away to appear at the home of a naughty child. The snow fell harder, almost whirling in the gusts. This was the strangest year. My mind continued to stay back with Thea and her daddy. I'd left them the switches, but they weren't real fuel. They were only good for starting a fire, and I couldn't remember how much, if any, firewood they had besides the few logs in the rack next to the woodstove.

I didn't recall any outside where I'd left the switches.

Or anywhere else.

Soon, I had stopped walking away and started walking in an ever-growing circle, gathering any downed branches or other wood. As soon as my arms were full, I'd haul them back to the porch and stack them then go back out again. It got harder and harder to find firewood, but I couldn't leave unless I knew they had what they needed for the duration of the blizzard.

The storm wasn't lessening in the slightest, and, with no guarantee how much longer I'd even be in the area, I needed to do more. A downed tree appeared in my path, one I'd swear hadn't been there before, although who could know for sure when even my enhanced vision couldn't make out what was more than a few feet in front of me.

It was only through the grace of Christmas Magic or whatever was guiding this weird night that I even found my way back to the house, dragging that log. That thirty-foot log. Plenty of wood for not only this storm but for weeks into the future.

If I could get it into manageable lengths.

The lights in the house had been turned out some time ago, and I didn't want to wake Jordan. Or his little girl. If not for the storm, they'd have heard me for sure. But this log wasn't going to do them any good lying down here half buried in the snow, so I looked around for something to get it cut down before I was swept away to my next stop.

And it had to be soon. Morning couldn't be that far away.

But although I slogged all the way around the house, I didn't see a shed or anything that was likely to hold a tool collection, and I was just about to give up when a thought occurred to me. The wood was definitely aged, and I'd managed to get it this far. Could I maybe handle it without tools?

I couldn't picture how that would work, but if it helped keep them warm, I'd give it my best try. I had my fist lifted to punch that log when I spotted a door leading under the porch.

The tool shed. Inside, I found an axe and a saw...anything a Krampus could need to split wood and prepare it for the stove. Which was so lucky because I probably would have broken every bone in my hand.

Christmas Magic notwithstanding.

It took me what remained of the night to saw that huge log into lengths I could split for firewood. But by the time I was done, I had a mountain of chunks of wood to haul onto the porch. I didn't know precisely but guessed I'd managed at least two cords of wood that night. That weird, weird night.

Then, unable to think of anything else to do, I turned my back on that little house on the side of the mountain and walked away. The sun would be rising soon, my night was over, and I hadn't done a single bit of Krampus work—Thea's very minor naughtiness aside. I couldn't pretend it wasn't a huge relief, but in a way this was so much worse.

I'd managed to find a level of peace in my life at the North Pole, but my evening sipping cocoa with Jordan and Thea had shattered that. They'd reminded me of what a regular happy life with people who cared for one another could be.

With each step, I put more distance between me and that night.

But at least tomorrow would be St. Nicholas Day.

Maybe I could catch a lift home.

Chapter Nine

Jordan

I woke up, chilled to the bone. My initial reaction was to pull the cover over my head like I did as a child, but then it all came rushing back to me—the storm, the power outage, Thea going missing, Krampus.

Noel and Noelle were curled up on the end of the bed all nestled together. "It's getting-up time," I told them.

They paid me no mind, all snug and warm.

I climbed out of bed and hurried down the stairs. If I was chilled, Thea would be, too, and, after her time in the cold last night, that could easily lead to getting sick, and that was the last thing she needed. A quick peek in her room to see her sleeping away and a quick trip to the bathroom later and I was ready to face the heating challenges.

Once downstairs, I went to work on stoking the fire to discover it needed to be completely relit. I was going to need to sleep downstairs until the heat came back on. It was easy to forget that the power was out. Between the lights working in the kitchen and the refrigerator running, it could so easily feel like we were just being cautious with saving electricity. That was until the cold hit.

"I need to get one of those pellet stoves," I grumbled as I tried to light the kindling again. Not that a pellet stove was a great solution. It, too, had its issues, but right now I just wanted to be warm.

Unlike last night, the flame came easily, and I sat back on my heels wanting to be sure that it was going strong before adding some more fuel to the fire.

Thea and I had a tradition of lighting the woodstove every Christmas Eve for ambiance. It was pretty to watch as the flames crackled. There was a time when she'd be cross we had a woodstove instead of a fire place. She'd been worried that not being able to hang the stockings there would be an issue.

It never was. I made sure of it.

After Krampus left and my heart calmed from the horror of almost losing my little girl, I somehow managed to get to sleep. Not a fitful sleep that had me waking every few seconds, but a deep sleep with a beautiful dream.

I dreamt of Christmas often during the years. The dreams were always the same: Christmas morning and everything is perfect from a gorgeous tree to presents underneath, fresh-fallen snow, and homemade cinnamon rolls. I was happy, so very happy. But then it would change. I'd go upstairs to wake up my mate, Theo, and he was gone, only to have the dream transformed to his funeral.

Last night? Last night it was different. In last night's dream, the cabin was decorated with garland and the dogs were wearing bandanas with Christmas trees; the cat was curled up in the window. There were homemade marshmallows and cocoa on the table with mugs for everyone, including Trudy, waiting for the others to wake up.

Shortly after, Thea came running down the stairs, Trudy in her arms, giggling that Santa had been here and asking me when he was coming. She never clarified who *he* was, but I knew. It was Krampus. We were waiting for Krampus.

And it filled me with joy.

I waited for the guilt to come, the guilt of it being okay that Theo wasn't here, the guilt of having maybe moved on more than I realized. It never did. I was probably just overthinking things. It was only a dream after all.

I put a few more pieces of wood into the stove. I had enough for a few hours but not enough for the day.

Standing up, I brushed off my knees and went outside to gather the last bits off the porch so I could dust the snow off of them and bring them in. The cord of wood I ordered was coming at the end of the month. It wasn't going to do me much good now. I was going to have to gather some more wood if this continued too long. At least there were tons of trees.

"Hey, you guys. Ready to go out?" The two dogs appeared at my side as I reached the door. I hadn't even noticed them coming down the stairs.

The sun was just beginning to rise, the weather colder than before, the snow slowing. "Now hurry up." I wasn't sure if I was going to need to shovel for them with the extra accumulation since last night, but they managed.

Confident they were fine, I went to grab the wood, only it wasn't just some wood, like had been there the night before. There was a ton of wood. Enough for a week of heat.

"Krampus," I said to myself and then cupped around my mouth and called out, "Thank you, Krampus." He didn't respond, of course he didn't. He'd gone back to the North Pole, and we'd never see him again unless Thea got really truly naughty and that was not only in her nature, but it was something I very much didn't want to see.

"Back inside, you two." Noel and Noelle didn't need to be asked twice, walking as fast as their little legs could carry them through the door, me following behind with an armload of wood that I left in the entrance.

"Morning, Daddy. Want a cheese sandwich?" Thea was at the table, loaf of bread and package of cheese in hand as if she hadn't snuck out, met a mythical creature that wasn't so mythical, and had only a few hours' sleep.

"Sure." I clicked the door close. "Thank you. When did you get up? Aren't you tired after last night?"

She shrugged and set the food on the table next to a couple of plates that were already there. Thea wanted to cook so badly, especially after watching a child's cooking competition on television. Sandwiches was our compromise for "cooking by herself." Consequently, we both ate a lot of sandwiches.

"I just got up. Can you grab me another plate?"

"You can't make the dogs sandwiches," I reminded her. "We've talked about human food not always being good for them."

"It's not for the dogs, Daddy. It's for you."

"You already have two plates." I pointed them out.

"This one is for Krampus," she said adamantly.

"He's not her honey, he had to go home." As much as I wished it weren't so.

"I think the sleigh left him, Daddy. Do you want a sandwich?" She laid the bread on the two plates, and I grabbed a third while trying to wrap my mind around this conversation.

"Here." I set it in front of her. "What makes you think he was left behind?" Please don't let it be because he was nice to us.

"I saw him from my window." She kept working on making her breakfast as if she hadn't just left a bombshell.

"Thea, I need you to listen to me carefully." She looked up and met my eyes. "You need to stay here and not leave this house."

She squeed and ran to me, throwing her arms around me. "You're going to get him, right, Daddy? You're going to get our Krampus."

Our. He sure felt like ours, and that should probably terrify me.

"Promise me," I ordered in a much sterner tone than usual—but I had to be sure she would obey.

“I promise, Daddy. Do you think he likes mayo on his sandwiches?”

“Sure.” I let go of her and got on my boots and coat. I had a Krampus to find.

Possibly our Krampus.

Chapter Ten

Alger

I didn't get a ride.

I'd been waiting all night to be whisked away to either my next stop or back to the North Pole. Even for me, it was cold, although the blizzard had moved on, the wind dying and the snowfall lessening. Back home, I didn't spend a heck of a lot of time outside, except when I was fishing and then wore whatever the latest was in cold weather gear. One thing Santa did not scrimp on was the shop where elves and others could pick out anything they liked for outdoor comfort.

For my first couple of decades, I'd been shunned from this facility, but when I staged a revolt and refused to share fish with the high table, Santa's hubby stepped in and insisted I receive equal treatment in the parka department. After all, it wasn't as if my job paid a salary allowing me to order my own. Even if the usual delivery services did bring shipments to our village.

So in whatever magical way Santa provided for the others, high-tech winter gear in my size appeared on the shelves, enabling me to sit comfortably on the bank of one of the lakes or in my hand-hewn folding chair—hewn by me—while I caught the bounty the Arctic provided.

On this night, however, I wore only a pair of thin leggings and a cloak in a horrible caricature of Santa's outfit. Not a huge issue since I was moving from place to place and the hideous Krampus body handled the cold better than the average human. Even my feet—I insisted on calling them beet despite their resemblance to hooves. Okay...they were hooves.

But on this strange night, I hadn't moved from place to place terrifying children. Instead, I'd spent the small hours filling the porch of the kind family who'd shared cocoa with me with firewood. And as the sky reluctantly lightened on the morn of St. Nicholas Day, I stood shivering before the little house and observed the results of my labors.

After the huge log, I'd waited a while for a magical shifting to another location, scanned the skies for the sleigh, and finally returned to my wood collecting. I'd run out of porch after the thirty-foot log, but the forest had yielded more, and with the late-rising winter sun peeking skeptically down on us both, I was facing enough wood for an elf colony in a polar winter—an unusually cold one.

And still no ride home. Christmas Magic had stranded me on the side of a mountain somewhere I didn't recognize and couldn't name but was fairly certain was in either the United States or Canada. A Krampus, a hideous terrifying beast, spent his night of mayhem collecting firewood for a family he had no business even associating with much less wishing he could go back inside and spend more time with.

Little Thea was a charmer, adorable and sweet but with a sassy side that would probably get her in trouble from time to time. You could see that spark in her eyes. Unlike the kids I was sent to torment, she had just enough fire. Exactly the right amount. She would go far in life.

But her father, Jordan... I had no business having the kinds of thoughts that cast graphic images in my mind while I built their woodpile for life. He was H.O.T. and watching how he cared for his child, even the way he treated me, a visitor from most people's nightmares as if I was just another guest who'd done a kindness to their family...how could I not fall for him.

Just a little.

Because it was pointless, and he could never know.

Would never know.

I plopped on the bottom step, sending a cloud of snow fluffing around me. If I didn't disappear soon, I'd have to just walk into the woods. There were many rules for my persona, none of which were written down or explained to me when I landed in the job but all of which I'd had a hundred years to figure out. And the one I felt most confident of was: Don't be in the human world roaming around in daylight.

And yet...here I was.

I stood and brushed off my bottom, ready to head away into the wilds before I was spotted. But then I heard him, the hot man. "Come inside and eat. We have cheese sandwiches, courtesy of Thea, and I'll make pancakes and bacon." All my good intentions for going off alone to wander maybe forever in the wilderness fell away.

"I haven't had pancakes in a century."

He chuckled. "That's a long time. I hope mine will be worth the wait." I turned to see him wearing sleep pants, his robe loosely belted at the waist to reveal a tantalizing glimpse of bare chest. "By the way, did you fill our porch with wood?"

"Also under the porch."

He leaned over the railing, and his jaw dropped. "You did all that since we last saw you?"

"It was a long winter's night." I grinned then suppressed it figuring it just made me look even worse to expose all those sharp teeth.

"Well, you must be very hungry. Please hurry and come in. Thea is waiting for you."

If this was a dream, I hoped I never woke up.

Following Jordan inside, I prayed that Christmas Magic, or whoever controlled it, wouldn't suddenly realize their mistake and whisk me back to the North Pole before I had breakfast. Thea was still wearing her Christmas jammies, Jordan in his smexy robe and sleep pants, and the stove glowed with warmth from the fire I'd helped to supply.

"Krampus!" She looked up from arranging quartered cheese sandwiches on plates, her smile blooming on her face in an expression no child had turned my way since the elf/cookie incident. My heart squeezed. "You came. I knew you wouldn't go away."

Well, that made one of us.

"I was invited to breakfast." I couldn't stop my response, and, judging from the fact she raced over to fling her arms around my waist, this little girl didn't find my smile too scary at all.

"Okay, you two." Jordan clapped his hands. "Sit down and eat your appetizers while I get the pancakes started." He winked. "Who wants bacon?"

My hand shot up just as fast as Thea's, but we insisted on helping, and soon the little house was redolent with the scent of maple bacon frying and we were competing on making pancake shapes. Jordan produced a bag of raisins for making snowman faces, and also, at Thea's insistence, dogs and cats and, in honor of my visit, a "North Pole" shape with the stripes done in chocolate syrup. Not traditional but effective.

The clouds had lifted while we cooked, revealing at least patches of pale-blue sky, the trees were white with snow as was the landscape, and we sat around the table eating and laughing almost like a real family. The hot daddy, the sweet, funny child, and me...Krampus of the hooves and fangs and distorted features.

But my companions treated me like a welcome guest.

It had to be a dream.

Chapter Eleven

Jordan

We ate pancakes until we couldn't eat another bite, and then Krampus asked Thea if there was possibly another cheese sandwich because it had been his favorite part of the meal.

Watching her face light up had been everything, and she, of course, ran to make him "the bestest cheese sandwich ever" and even cut it into triangles for him to make it fancy. Not once had she looked at him as the scary beast with hooves, fangs, and horns. He was her Krampus, and she adored him.

But really, I didn't see any of him as scary, either, not once I knew she was safe. If anything, I longed to touch him and not because he was attractive. It wasn't anything like that. It was more because there was this connection between us, this connection that shouldn't be there.

I couldn't help but feel like he was stuck because of us. That his helping save my daughter was the reason he couldn't go home.

"Thea, why don't you go upstairs and clean your room while I do the dishes?" I don't know why I asked. It wasn't really a question at all.

"But Krampus is here. We have company. It would be rude."

"Rude to give him a tour of the house in a little while and have him see your messy room," I countered, and she took off like a flash up the stairs.

"I can help with the dishes." Krampus stood up from his spot and started to stack them.

"You don't have to. You're a guest. Hold on while I check the fire, and maybe we can figure out all of...well, this." I swished my arm in the air in a huge circle.

I went over to the fire and made sure it was good, so grateful I didn't have to worry about firewood. Krampus did that. He hadn't had to, and I was downright sure he wasn't supposed to, but he did, and why? Because he had such kindness inside of that teeth-filled, horned body. He was a good man...beast. He was good. Full stop.

Back in the kitchen area, the dishes were piled up by the sink and the table cleaned completely off. He was quick, his clawed hands really agile. Only they didn't seem as claw-like as they had last night. Maybe I was getting used to his aesthetic.

"You didn't have to do all that." I grabbed a pot and filled it with water then put it on the gas stove to heat it. I could have put it on the woodstove like I did the tea kettle, but it would have taken longer. "The water heater is out with the electricity," I explained.

"But you have lights?" He quirked his head.

"I have a very small generator that does a few things, including the refrigerator and some random lights. It's quite handy," I added quickly, not wanting him to think I was woefully unprepared for life. "I have a large generator, too, but it is waiting on a part. This is...it's unusual that I'm having to live by firewood and cold water."

"Everything is quite unusual," he agreed, rubbing the side of his nose with the back of his hand.

"Speaking of which, why are you here?" It came out wrong, and I could see he heard it as such. I wanted to immediately take it back, but it was too late, hurt crossing his eyes.

"I can leave." He started to turn to leave, but I put my hand on his arm, not to restrain him—there was no way I could, even if it was my intent. No, I wanted him to feel my words.

"Please don't. I didn't mean it like that at all. I like you here...when you left... Anyway, I just wanted to know how you got stuck. Why did they leave you? Was it because you helped us?"

He just blinked up at me for a few seconds before answering. "I don't know."

"I just thought Krampus comes one day a year, and you are here two now, but maybe that was wrong, too, like the part about you snatching children and beating them with switches and eating dogs."

He gasped. "Humans think we eat dogs? How can they get everything so wrong?"

My hand was still on his arm, and I made no move to remove it, loving the warmth coming from our connection.

"We get a lot of things wrong. But the one-day thing, it was right, wasn't it. That's why you were wandering around this morning, late last night?" He leaned into my touch.

"Yes. But I don't know why I was here or why they didn't come get me or any of it. I didn't even have a child to scare."

"Do you usually have a lot of visits to make?"

He shook his head slightly.

"Then are there a lot of you?" I hadn't thought of that before. In the books, there were a bunch of them, but given I'd read he ate pet dogs, that didn't mean anything.

"I don't know." Meaning, he didn't know any like him. Loneliness shone in his eyes. Poor guy.

Meow. Cookie had come down from her warm bed at some point and was now rubbing herself against Krampus's leg. He bent to pet her, and my hand fell from his arm. I wanted to reach back over and regain the connection.

"You missed the bacon, Cookie." He laughed. "I'd have given you some, too, just ask your dogs."

I, too, joined in on the laughter. One thing was sure—no pet went unspoiled in this house.

The pot came to a boil, and I filled the sink with hot sudsy water and added the dishes while Krampus gave Cookie the attention she outright demanded.

The thought of him leaving caused an inexplicable ache deep inside me, but he needed to go. Thea and I saw him for who he was, but others wouldn't. They would scream and run from him or try to harm him or worse. They might confine him in a lab for a scientific study. No. He needed to return to the North Pole, even if the life he led hadn't sounded particularly nice so far, except for the marshmallows.

"I could learn to make marshmallows," I said to myself, not realizing I'd spoken the words aloud until Krampus responded.

"They are not easy. But I bet you could do it. There will be a big Marshmallow Festival up there tomorrow." He was now sitting on the floor, Cookie on his lap.

I'd thought about monsters a lot as a kid. They were in closets, under beds, and outside if you stayed up too late. I even drew quite a few with my big fat crayons, the ones I loved best even when I was far too old to be using them. But not one had I envisioned one sitting criss-cross applesauce with a cat on his lap.

"What's so special about tomorrow?" I asked, scrubbing away. Once the water got cold, it was cold. I still had a half a pot on the stove for rinsing, but if I took too long, it would all be cold.

"To celebrate a successful St. Nicholas, of course. It's not as grand as the cookie festival on the day after Christmas. Or so I've heard. I've not been invited to either."

I was really starting to hate the North Pole. How could they treat such a sweet and compassionate being that way. “What about hitching a ride home tonight? When he comes to fill the shoes?” I asked. It sounded as logical as anything.

“Do you do that in this house?” It was a fair question. Not all people did celebrate the day in any way.

“No. But we could.”

I rinsed off the dishes and called Thea downstairs.

“Thea, what do you know about St. Nicholas Day?”

Chapter Twelve

Alger

After a day of more than pleasant companionship with my host and young hostess, I was more than grateful for the delay. Only Christmas Magic knew when I'd have another opportunity to feel like a person again.

If someone had asked, I'd have sworn I'd gotten over the loneliness my position gave me, but I had to recognize that I hadn't, I'd just suppressed it. Mostly so I didn't ache all the time. Having nobody in my life except an elf who actually cursed me and now liked to drink cocoa or occasionally tea with me did not make for a fulfilling existence.

Thea's laughter reminded me of good times long, long ago. She'd been tucked into bed hours ago, exhausted by a day of being a normal, adorable child. Nearly twenty-four hours in her company had me even more sure that I'd been set down here by mistake. My only question was whether Christmas Magic could even locate me because if it could, I'd have been whisked away to all my previously scheduled visits and by now be back home in my little shack above the Arctic Circle.

By dinnertime, when we were all eating bowls of hearty stew accompanied by flaky biscuits, I had been having a hard time suppressing the flicker of hope deep in my icy heat that maybe I wouldn't have to go back at all. A ridiculous idea because Krampus must go on, and how could I possibly continue to exist here in the mortal world in my current state?

It wasn't as if I could just wander into the supermarket and hoof it down the aisle. Drop off Thea at school and visit with all the other fathers who were doing the same. "So where do you get your fangs polished?"

"Is it hard to find dress shoes for your hooves?"

"Is your family as scared of you as we all are?"

No, I had to leave as soon as possible and accept that this interlude was just some sort of glitch that accidentally gave me a break from my miserable existence. Nobody would want a Krampus as a mate.

Mate? Where did that thought even come from?

No, all I had from this experience was the best day, one I'd have to remember forever.

The topic had come up about whether there were other Krampuses. And truth...I didn't know. If there were, I'd never run into one, but I didn't mingle in the village a lot. If there were, maybe we could get together and have dinner sometime, share our misery.

If I wasn't the only one...and if I didn't ever get picked up and returned...would someone else have to take care of my "clients" next year? Had they, in fact, done it last night?

With Jordan also gone to bed, I was curled up on the couch with a quilt over me, waiting for St. Nicholas to arrive. Thea had left her shoes out to be filled, and to my understanding, if a child did that, he had to stop by and fill them. Like me and my scary visits, it was part of the whole deal.

Santa, St. Nicholas, Sinterklaas...unlike me, Santa had many faces depending on where he was found in the world. But for sure only one actual being handling all that. If there was more than one, the elves would be talking about it. Krampus...they tried to pretend I didn't exist. Most of the children I'd known were waiting for the big guy on Christmas Eve, but on the saint's feast day, he was expected to show up in some areas to fill shoes with presents. The shoes would do it. In all the pictures, they were wooden shoes or something like that, but Thea's sneakers with the light-up toes should fit the bill just fine.

"You still awake?" Jordan's voice from behind me was no less appealing in whisper form. Maybe even more, judging by the tingle down my twisted spine.

"Oh yes. I didn't want to fall asleep and miss my ride." My chuckle sounded awkward even to me. "You've had to put up with me long enough, I'm afraid."

"It's not like that." He dropped a hand on my shoulder and gave it a pat. I didn't breathe, wanting it to stay there, adding this memory to all the others of this day. But, to my disappointment, he gave my shoulder a squeeze and then lifted his hand. "Want some company while you wait? I can make tea."

I probably should have said no, but the words coming from my mouth were, "That sounds great if it's not too much trouble."

"Not at all. I can't sleep, either. And who knows? Maybe I'll get a glimpse of St. Nick." Jordan moved into the kitchen area and filled the kettle, got out the tea caddy, etc.

"Sure, everyone knows Santa is the star of the Christmas season," I mumbled, trying not to be miffed that Jordan would be happier for a glimpse of St. Nick than all the time he'd spent with me. Of course, who wouldn't be? Jolly happy soul with his beaming smile compared to the twisted, horrifying thing even now ensconced under a handmade quilt on Jordan's couch.

"Did you say something?"

"Uh...I take it black."

"I remember." He smiled before he turned back to continue getting everything ready.

Of course he remembered. I'd been here all day and had a few cups of tea. So I shouldn't be glad that he knew how I liked mine. It wasn't because I was special. Just that he noticed things. Ordinary things.

Jordan set the tray with the cups and other things on the coffee table and then returned to get the kettle and set it on top of the woodstove. He had a regular stove in the kitchen, but I'd noticed he liked to use the other one to boil water for tea. See? I knew something about him, too. Actually I'd memorized everything he did so I could replay it in my head in my day and night dreams when I was back at the North Pole where everyone pretty much treated me like crap.

I shrugged all of that off, not wanting it to taint the rest of what little time I had left before I had to leave. When the kettle sang, I got up and grabbed a hot pad and then filled our cups where the teabags were already waiting. "So, tell me what the two of you will be up to for Christmas while I'm at the North Pole again."

"Oh." He looked stricken, and I remembered something he'd told me earlier and wished I hadn't asked. "It's not my favorite time of the year anymore. But I try to make it good for Thea."

"Your mate died around now in that accident, didn't he? Several years ago?"

He nodded, taking the teabag out of his cup and setting it on the folded paper towel beside it. "Yes. He loved Christmas so much. Always made a huge deal about it with tons of decorations and parties and little thoughtful gifts. Not expensive, necessarily. We weren't rich, but we felt like we were, you know?"

"Because you were happy together." It wasn't a question. The love for his mate, taken too soon, still lurked in his eyes. Would anyone ever feel that way about me? When I'd disappeared from my world, way back when, had anyone even noticed?

"We were. And for a long time, I let other people try to help us, me and Thea, find happiness again by joining their holiday instead of making our own. This is the first time we're flying without a net."

"Little scary?" I removed my teabag and sat back, cradling the mug. "I know I would be frightened." Then I barked a laugh. "But I guess if you're not afraid of me, you're not afraid of much."

He scooted back to sit next to me and rested his head on my arm. "It's not the same at all. You're kind. You saved my daughter. And you're sitting here listening to me without judgment. Without trying to fix everything. Our family and friends meant well, but I think this year they figured out we needed to move forward on our own."

"Christmas is hard." Without a net. I got it. And as I sat there with that amazing, brave man, talking about everything and nothing, my eyes got heavy, and before I knew it, sweet darkness enfolded me in a restful sleep. Maybe the first one in a hundred years.

Chapter Thirteen

Jordan

I woke up snug and warm, an arm wrapped around me. I didn't miss it—miss saying good-bye to my Krampus.

"Sorry, I fell asleep." I let out a long yawn. "I'm glad I didn't miss you leaving. I wanted to say goodbye."

His arm tightened around me and then retracted, as if my arm was made of fire, and I sat up like a shot. "I'm so sorry. I didn't mean...I fell asleep and I'm sorry I made you uncomfortable." I slid over on the couch.

"No. You didn't. That felt good it's just..." He pointed to where the shoes had been so carefully lined up, complete with note for St. Nicholas. "He didn't leave anything in the shoes. He took them."

"Who's he? St. Nicholas? I bet the dogs just moved them." I got off the couch and started to look around for the shoes but saw no evidence of them whatsoever.

"The dogs have been cuddled on the other side of me since I sat down," he said and, sure enough, there they sat, Cookie on the back of the couch behind his head. "Your pets seem to like me." He forced a chuckle.

"We all do," I said in all seriousness. "But that doesn't answer the question about the shoes. Where could they have gone?"

"Ernie," he mumbled under his breath. "If this was Ernie, I'm never going to forgive him." He stood up, the cat looking beyond miffed to lose her companion.

"Who's Ernie?" I wasn't quite sure I wanted to know.

"You don't want to know. Let's just say he's an elf who won't earn my forgiveness a second time around."

"See?" Thea interrupted. She was hanging out with Cookie too much. I hadn't even heard her climbing down the steps. "Elves are scary."

I squatted down in front of her. "Thea, do you know where your shoes are?" I asked. "The ones we left for St. Nicholas?"

"Come with me." She sprinted up the stairs, stopping at the landing to hurry us along.

We followed her up, both Krampus and I as well as Cookie who'd become his official shadow.

"See!" She was bouncing up and down on her bed, Trudy propped up by her pillow with two doll shoes in front of her, and Thea's sitting right in front of those filled with I wasn't sure what from my angle. "He came and he brought something for Trudy. Trudy gets left out a lot on account of being a doll, so this was pretty spectacular. St. Nicholas day is the king of loopholes."

I was pretty sure she didn't understand what loopholes were, but that wasn't my concern. The filled shoes—up here and away from where we'd been waiting for Krampus's ride were.

"I'm sorry. I didn't think she would move the shoes." I took Krampus's hand. "We'll figure this out." I wasn't sure how, but we would.

He might not deserve the lonely life he had at the North Pole, but no one deserved the life he'd have to lead here. He'd either have to hide with us all of the time and hope the mailman didn't catch a glimpse of him or be in peril every second of the day. Neither of those were acceptable to me, but, if given the choice, him being safe won out every time.

"I figured it out before I moved the shoes."

My gaze went straight to her. I started to count in my head, not wanting to let out the words I was feeling. She'd ruined things for Krampus. There was no acceptable reason for her to move the shoes and, given they were in my sight before I fell asleep, she snuck down in the middle of the night to do so.

"Little one, why did you trap me here?" Krampus's voice cracked and, with it, my heart.

"I didn't trap you here. I left a note in the shoe. I asked St. Nicholas if I could have more time with you. Said I'd miss you if you were gone, and this was my first happy Christmas in a long time." She fished through the shoes, pulled out a piece of paper, and climbed off her bed to bring it to him.

"Thea. How could you?" There were so many feels floating through me. I had no idea Christmas hadn't been happy for her. I'd worked so hard to make it so, but I'd failed. I'd failed her, and now I'd failed Krampus. And even with that, part of me was happy, happy he'd be with us as wrong as that was.

"You're welcome." She hugged me tight. "You like him, too. You smiled so much yesterday."

"This note—" Krampus interrupted. "It was in your shoe?"

"Uh-huh. I wrote my letter and went to put it in the shoe for him to find, and I saw an elf. He was going to steal the note and make you go. I snatched those shoes so fast and ran upstairs. I was safe. Cookie was in my room then, and elves hate cats." I had no idea where she got that from, but that was the least of my worries right then.

“What did the elf look like?” For the very first time, I saw how scary Krampus could be. He was very displeased, not at Thea from what I could gather but the elf.

“They don’t matter...read the note.”

He unfolded the paper. “Krampus, be ready Christmas Eve.”

“See. You can stay.” She ran to him and jumped into his arms, Krampus stumbling as if unsure of what was happening. “You can stay and help me color in my new book St. Nicholas left. It has a Krampus but not a mean one in it. A Krampus like you.”

“Thea, why don’t you go brush your teeth and get ready for the day? I need to talk to Krampus and figure this all out.”

“Okay, but don’t start coloring without me.” She climbed down and scampered off.

“I’m so sorry.” I apologized as soon as she left the room. “If I had even suspected, I’d have made sure to put a bell on her door or something.”

“Don’t you see? She saved me from being stuck here.” He handed me the note. “She wrote the letter, and now I know I have a ride. If she hadn’t snuck out, that elf would've snatched those shoes so quick, and where would we be."

"The elf…that wasn't her imagination?" He shook his head. "There was an elf here trying to trap you?" This time a nod. "Why would he do that?"

"Because I took his cookie."

Chapter Fourteen

Alger

When Thea hid her shoes, I couldn't be mad. I really couldn't be mad at Ernie, either. Not really. After all, what did I have to go back to but more of the same. I was also a little worried about what I might face when I got there. Whatever glitch had placed me on that frozen hillside on the night of my arrival was not my fault.

Or was it?

Since nobody had ever explained to me how it truly worked, I couldn't know for sure if I'd done something to throw things off. Maybe I'd had a bad thought or leaned in the wrong direction during transport. It had never happened before, but Christmas Magic was spoken of only in the most hushed tones by the elves in the streets of the village, and I didn't get the impression they understood much about it, either.

"Krampus! Are you ready? It's time to build a snowman!" Thea was bouncing up and down as if on springs, her eyes sparkling and mittened hands clapping together. "Daddy said we would build a snowman today. We need a carrot and some lumps of coal for his eyes and some cookies for his buttons."

All bundled up in her snowsuit and boots, head covered with her pompom hat, the little girl was about the cutest thing I'd ever seen. But some things I just could not do. "Thea, you can look in the refrigerator for a carrot, and if you haven't snuck all the cookies while you thought your daddy and I weren't looking—"

She opened her mouth to deny it, but I flashed her a stern look. "With Christmas Eve right around the corner, are you going to tell a fib to Krampus? Because it might be past my day, but Santa still has his ways for those on his naughty list."

"Coal?" Her lower lip was thrust outward in an adorable pout. "He has coal."

"Right, and if you really want it instead of toys, fibbing is the best way to get it."

"I didn't eat *all* the cookies." Her gaze was cast downward, watching her booted toe draw circles on the floor.

"Most?"

"Maybe we can make his buttons out of something else? Like little rocks?"

Jordan was upstairs putting away some laundry, so we spent a little time designing our snowman's features. With the power back on, the washer and dryer were running full-time on catch-up. By the time he came downstairs, we had laid out our pattern on the kitchen counter.

"Look, Daddy. The snowman's going to have a carrot nose." She tilted her head up to look at him. "That's traditional." She was so serious, I had to suppress a chuckle. "And we don't have any coal." She lowered her voice. "The only way we could come up with getting some was from Santa if I told a fib so we went 'nother way."

He cast me a questioning glance, and I shrugged. Thea had all of this in hand. "So what did you decide to use for his eyes and mouth?"

"Craisins." She wrinkled her nose. "They're smaller so we have to use more than one. But they are the right color." And she'd been glad to use them up. Not her favorite dried fruit. "And prunes for buttons. Because we don't have enough cookies." Two. We had two cookies.

"Do you have a hat for him? And a scarf?"

Her grin stretched across her face. "We made them out of cardboard and with markers. Krampus did the cutting part because I'm not 'llowed to use the big scissors."

"Sounds like you two don't even need me." He pretended to walk away, but Thea threw her arms around his knees.

"We need you because we love you."

I choked on my strangled breath. We. Love. You. Something I hadn't dared to even allow myself to entertain. What would he say? Would he think I told her that I loved him? That I was trying to horn in on their family when I was just a guest until Christmas Eve when I would have to return with Santa Claus?

But, to my relief, Jordan didn't seem to notice her inclusion of me in the statement. He peeled her off and sent her to put back on all the outerwear she'd shed while we were working on our design in the warm kitchen. "I'm not sure I have the artistic ability to work with you two, but I'm willing to be the grunt."

"We really do need you," I said, wishing I could finish the statement as Thea had but instead making a joke. "This snowman is going to be 'epic,' to quote your daughter, and someone has to help make the giant snowballs."

We all bundled up, me less than the others, since I didn't have a lot to bundle into and had the most cold tolerance. But I did bend down to allow Thea to wrap a woolly scarf around my neck and press a kiss to my cheek that chipped away even more of the ice around my heart.

That was probably not good since it was the only thing protecting me from the pain of living day to day up there in the far reaches of Santa's realm, but I couldn't hold her at bay. The beauty of this season would have to keep me going for who knew how long. Maybe centuries. Okay...way to get maudlin. Way to waste precious moments.

Crushing the negativity under my hoof, I followed Jordan and Thea and the two dogs outside to begin creating our masterpiece under the supervision of our little design chief.

Jordan and I together made a snowball we figured was big enough for the base. Thea declared it the perfect size for the head. By the time we'd finished rolling the balls and stacking them, I had to put the little girl on my shoulders for her to decorate the snowman's face.

Our cardboard hat and scarf would not last long outdoors, but since a few little birds were already on a branch nearby eyeing our dried fruit features, I figured it wouldn't be the only thing to go. But we could always come up with an alternative to replace anything that became a snack, and this little girl, who loved animals, wouldn't mind if some hungry winter bird got something to eat.

Finally, we all stood back and admired our work. "He looks beautiful," pronounced Thea.

And we all agreed before tromping back into the house to divest ourselves of all the extra clothes and stand by the window drinking cocoa and continuing to admire our snowman who already had one eye and a button missing.

"Those birdies were hungry, Daddy," she pronounced. "We need to give them seeds."

And so it was decided that the very next day, we'd build a bird feeder.

Nearly all the ice was gone from my heart, and when this was over, I might not survive the raw pain of loneliness and loss.

But for now, I'd take every bit of happiness and love this house and its inhabitants shared with me.

Love? Yes, I loved them both but too much to tell them so.

Chapter Fifteen

Jordan

"Why do I have to go to school? We only have Krampus for another week." She was sitting on her bed, her arms crossed.

"Because the roads are cleared and if you don't go, it's considered being truant." I sat down beside her. "You know what truant means?"

"It's when Jasper won't go to school because he wants to play video games and Mr. Simon has to go to his house and go get him." My jaw nearly dropped. How could a classroom with kids her age already have students who needed the principal to go get them?

"Yes, that. And if Mr. Simon comes here, what will he see?" Her eyes went wide with terror. Being up on the side of the mountain so completely hidden away had us able to just be and not worry about Krampus being seen. Playing hooky, that was a different thing altogether.

"They could come and hurt Krampus." She got up and off the bed. "That wouldn't be worth it. I'll go to school and even do my work."

"You always do your work," I reminded her.

"Of course I do. If I don't, Trudy isn't allowed to recess." She grabbed her doll off the bed. "I better go get my quantity time with Krampus before we need to go."

"Quality time? That means really worthwhile time. Quantity means a lot." I stood up, ready to walk down with her.

"I already got us some quantity time." She waggled her finger at me. "You need to get us more. It's almost Christmas, and I don't have any more ideas."

The sadness in her little face as she tried to take control of the situation…it was almost too much.

"We'll figure something out, honey. We will." I just didn't know how, but she was right. We were running out of time and rapidly. "Let's get you breakfast."

"I'll race you."

She won. I didn't even pretend to sprint. I needed a few minutes to pull myself together. When I got downstairs, she was eating her oatmeal, and Krampus was telling her all the fun things they could do when she got home. It looked like there were some crafts in my future and a whole lotta glitter.

"I'll be back in a bit. It sounds like I need to stop at the store on my way to get supplies."

"I'll be here." He smiled back at me. Maybe it was the amount of time we'd been spending together or maybe it was the lighting, but his toothy grin looked less deadly and more sweet today than it ever had. I wanted to reach over and kiss him. I didn't, of course. Not only was it inappropriate, but we had an impressionable audience.

Dropping Thea off was easier than I feared it might be. She wanted to keep him safe, to protect him, and if that meant going to school and missing some "quantity" time, she was all for it. She was such a strong little alpha already.

I did stop at the store for gobs of craft supplies and some odds and ends that caught my eye. On my way back, I made a spontaneous trip through a fast-food place for breakfast. Krampus had spent one night a year down with the humans for around a hundred years. I imagined none of them included a trip for an egg sandwich and hash browns.

I drove up to my house where smoke billowed from the chimney, not because we needed the fire to keep us warm any more but because it was that kind of day. Noel and Noelle greeted me at the front door, doubly excited when they saw the red-and-white paper bag filled with food.

"None of this is for you, little ones. It has sausage, and I'm pretty sure your bellies wouldn't appreciate either that or the grease." They didn't like my answer.

I found Krampus in the kitchen, a bunch of things from the pantry on the table.

"Baking?" I guessed.

"Not really. This box has a recipe for marshmallows, so I thought I would give it a try." He held up a box of plain gelatin packets I'd picked up for a salad I never made.

"Well, if we are going to make something as fancy as that, best have full bellies first." I held up the bag of food.

"It smells good. What is it?" I set the bags of craft supplies on the counter and brought the bag over to him.

"This is fast food. It is really bad for you, has more grease and salt than you need in a week, and is quite possibly the most delicious breakfast food you will ever taste."

"It sounds...decadent."

"Monetarily, not so much. The burritos were only a dollar each." I'd pretty much picked up a variety. "So how about we eat all the bad-for-you breakfast food and then attempt the marshmallows?"

"I'm in."

We sat down and I made a show of it, explaining each item and cutting it into pieces for us to scientifically test which was better. In the end, we decided nothing other than they all needed to be eaten and enjoyed.

"Thank you. That was so...I don't want to say thoughtful because that doesn't feel adequate."

He was crumpling up wrappers and putting them into the bag for us to throw out.

"I never thought about experiencing things that are part of your world like this. I've been so happy just being here with you guys, and I don't know...I hadn't thought to venture out. Thank you."

I placed my hand on his. "They were greasy sandwiches that might possibly make your stomach hurt later, but you're welcome. And for the record, Thea isn't the only one happy to have you here."

I wanted to say more...so much more. But really, what good would it do us? We couldn't be together. It wasn't an option. I wasn't welcome in the world he lived in, and he wasn't welcome in ours. This place, it was a temporary in-between space where we could pretend. That's all it was though...pretend.

"Let's see if we can figure out these marshmallows and surprise Thea when she comes home.

We did not figure out the marshmallows and ended up with a sticky mess of I didn't even know what you could call it. It didn't even taste good. But we had a blast and a new mission to learn how to master the sugary delights.

"I vote we watch a tutorial video before I have to leave and get Thea," I said, tying up the bag with the evidence of our failings. "And maybe we can see the error of our ways for when we try again."

Maybe we could make enough marshmallows to buy Krampus a holiday or two here each year. Wouldn't that be everything?

Chapter Sixteen

Alger

"God rest ye merry, gentlemen, let nothing ye dismay..." The strains of holiday songs poured from the radio as we got the special dinner ready for Christmas Eve. Jordan and Thea had rearranged their holiday plans so they were doing everything on the Eve rather than Christmas morning. Oh, Santa's gifts would of course be a morning thing because he hadn't left them yet, but we'd all be exchanging with each other tonight.

If we didn't, there'd be no time to do it at all because when the jolly old saint dropped off those gifts, he'd be picking me up. As he'd said in his note, I'd be ready Christmas Eve. Ready to leave this family who had made me feel at home. I knew every inch of this little house like the back of my hand.

As the days and weeks passed, I had stopped being a guest and become someone who lived there, even though we all knew it was temporary. But if I didn't think too hard on it, I could go through all the household routines just like everyone else. I took my turns washing dishes and cooked, although I wasn't as good at it as Jordan. I swept and mopped and carried in wood for the fire.

Jordan didn't want his daughter to be tied to a screen when she was not in school. We did watch movies together in the evenings, sometimes, usually holiday themed, most often animated. But the rest of the time we worked on projects, like Christmas cookies or building a gingerbread house, even made little star ornaments for the tree out of Popsicle sticks and some yarn we found in the attic. And glitter. We made great use of the craft supplies, but it seemed each and every project was coated in the stuff. Since most of the video games and whatever kids did on their phones and other devices were well beyond my time—okay, all of them were—I wouldn't have known what to do with them anyway.

But I did like board games. Ernie was a fan and had brought some of his favorites with him from the toy workshop when he visited me, so when Jordan and Thea opened the cupboard under the stairs to reveal the collection left behind by the people before them, I was right there ready to compete. Some were age appropriate for Thea, some a little too advanced, but we had plenty to entertain ourselves as we waited for Santa.

We also had agreed to make gifts for one another rather than buying them. Of course, Jordan had brought some presents for Thea before I came here, but other than that, we were doing a homemade, old-fashioned holiday. A theme I believed was largely for my benefit since I had no money—not even pockets to put money in, and they wouldn't want me to feel bad if I didn't have something nice to give in exchange.

A great deal of whispering went on as the holiday drew near. Thea and Jordan, Jordan and me, Thea and me...all sharing secrets about what we were creating for the others. Thea occasionally needed help for things like the "big scissors" or gluing, but other than that, she had her own path and trod it decisively—with giggles.

"Do we have everything ready?" I studied the living room where the tree we'd cut down together stood proudly decorated with the Popsicle stick and yarn ornaments, strings of popcorn and cranberry, paper chains, and anything else that felt festive to us. There were a few cat toys on there because they were made of shiny foil that caught the light. And proudly, at the top, was a star made from more aluminum foil. We'd watched the YouTube video on how to create that at least a dozen times and gone through three boxes of foil before we all agreed it was perfect.

A tray of appetizers stood on the counter, three kinds. Jordan had chosen to make delicate puffs of crab and shrimp for his, I'd done little hot dogs rolled in croissant pastry, and, for her option, Thea had created a cracker topped with peanut butter, jelly, and a dab of cream cheese.

The scent of garlic-rubbed rib roast mingled with the fresh pine of the tree, and we would enjoy the roast with potatoes au gratin, fresh green beans sauteed with almonds, and soft dinner rolls. Jordan and Thea had gone to town to buy the fixings for our feast a couple of days before, apologizing over and over for not taking me with them, but I told them to stop. Terrorizing the town was not my idea of a fun shopping trip.

"Cocktail time!" Jordan announced, bringing a tray over to where Thea and I sat admiring the tree and discussing the possibilities of the packages wrapped in an assortment of anything but traditional wrapping paper. Grocery bags—paper and plastic—dish towels, ancient news print...it might not be colorful, but it was sincere.

Everything about our holiday was sincere.

And memorable.

I took mental pictures of it every few seconds.

When we all had cups of hot, spiced cider, I lifted my mug. “Let’s have a toast.”

They also raised their cups.

And then I had to think what to say because when you suggest the toast, it’s your job to give it. What words could possibly convey what I needed to express to these kind people?

“You opened your hearts and your home to a stranger—one who nearly anyone would have turned and run from at best, probably screaming. These two-plus weeks have been the best of my life, even counting before I became Krampus. I’m leaving in a few hours but I hope you will always remember me fondly as I will you.” My throat was tightening, and the words came harder and harder, but I desperately needed to get this out. There would not be another time. “I love you both and wish you many happy holidays in the future.” I lifted my cup to sip but Thea piped up.

“Angels underwear.”

Jordan and I both froze. “What did you say, Thea?” His eyes virtually bulged, although I didn’t really understand why.

“Angels underwear.”

"Oh, Thea. Do you mean Angels unawares?"

She bobbed her head so vigorously, the cider almost splashed over the top. "Yes. You have to have people come for Christmas because they are angels."

Even more confused, I turned to Jordan. His eyes were glossy, and he sniffed a little bit. "I take it you know what she means?"

"Yes, but I don't know how she knows. Her dad used to like to have people over for Christmas or whatever. Family and friends, of course, but whoever else needed a place for a holiday meal. When people commented about the homeless guy or the elderly lady he brought from her care home because someone said she was all alone, he would say that quote about angels unawares."

"I don't...what is it?"

"Be not forgetful to entertain strangers: for thereby some have entertained angels unawares." He wiped a droplet from his cheek. "But she can't possibly know what she's talking about. She must have heard it somewhere else."

"Wherever it came from, you lived it this year. And I'll always be grateful for you and the angels underwear."

We exchanged our homemade gifts, a hilarious collection mostly full of glitter, but Jordan and I kept our homemade "magic view glasses" on anyway, hoping not to be blinded, and our dinner was delicious. We put Thea to bed after dinner, against her protests of wanting more "quantity" time with me before I left.

She also had it figured out that Santa never came if the children of the house were still awake and seemed determined to use that as a last chance of keeping "her" Krampus. But her Krampus, aka me, gently tucked her in and thanked her for helping me stay with them as long as I had. Until I was released, if that ever happened, I had to go back to the North Pole.

"Like my school." She sighed. "But you don't have to go out again till next year."

"I know, baby, but duty calls. I have to spend my time at the North Pole. It's a rule." I kissed her forehead and went downstairs while her daddy finished tucking her in.

I was 100 percent with Thea. I'd do anything to stay here. But it wasn't meant to be.

Chapter Seventeen

Jordan

Something Krampus said wouldn't leave my head. Not as we sang, not as we ate, and not even as my sweet baby girl drifted off to sleep. *Even counting before I became Krampus.* I guess I had always assumed he just was. Born that way to ever remain that way. Thinking back, there had been little clues along the way, but I hadn't picked up on them.

"I don't know much about you," I admitted as we sat, watching the fire and waiting for his ride. There was none of the excitement I had as a child waiting for Santa. No, this time it was dread. Once Santa arrived, Krampus would be gone from my life.

"I suppose you don't." He leaned back against the couch. "Let me see if I can answer most things you probably wanted to ask but were too uncomfortable to." He took in a deep breath and let it out slowly. Then took in another.

"I don't need shoes like horses, they just magically are fine. My horns are hollow and not heavy. They could break, in theory, but never have. I don't know why my hands are more hand-like. I asked Ernie when he came, and he told me I was making it up, but I wasn't. I can touch you now without fearing I'll inadvertently hurt you. And then there's that, I suppose. I do want to touch you, and it's wrong or whatever, but I can't help how I feel." He opened his eyes and turned to face me. "Did that answer all of them?"

"None of those ever crossed my mind." I reached out and cupped his cheek. "Not a one, although now I'm wondering about this Ernie guy." Because as much as I didn't want to, I was jealous of him. Jealous he knew Krampus on a different level than I did. Jealous he was able to come and go here, and Krampus wasn't. And maybe that wasn't even jealousy, but it was something not good churning in my belly, and I hated it.

"Ernie might be an elf, but he's sort of my friend, too."

My hand dropped. An elf. In here. "Thea really saw an elf that night stealing her shoes. That wasn't her imagination?" On some level I always knew that, but this made it somehow more real.

"It was, and I have no idea why. He wouldn't tell me, but I can tell you with 100 percent certainty that he was only here because of me."

"Because he's your boyfriend?" My voice cracked, the sound of it coming from my lips painful.

"Hardly. He's barely even a friend, but out of all the people up there, he treats me the best."

"Oh." I should've asked him why the elf was here and why he hid it from me. I should've asked what the whole hands thing might mean. I should've asked him why he thought it was wrong to touch me. Instead, I asked him the only question that mattered.

"May I kiss you?" I asked already coming closer. We might only have a few hours or possibly minutes left, and I wanted to make the most of them. I'd never be able to forgive myself if I didn't let him know how I felt. "I've been wanting to for a while. I love you, and I know all the reasons we can't be. But maybe, just maybe could we have this?"

He pressed his forehead against mine. "I love you, too. I shouldn't. I shouldn't even be here, but I am, and I can't help how I feel."

"I'm going to kiss you now, before it's too late." I brought my lips to his and pressed a small kiss against them, only to snap back at the sound of little feet imitating an elephant on the stairs.

"He's here. Santa's here. Quick, hide."

"We can't hide, Thea. Santa is magic, remember?" Krampus said, his hand now holding mine. "There's nothing we can do."

She climbed up onto both of our laps.

"I can tell Santa, 'No.' No is a complete sentence, you know."

"And one that won't keep you on the nice list," Krampus reminded her.

"Good, because if I'm on the naughty list, then even if he takes you, you get to come back to us." She hugged his arm. "Daddy, tell Krampus he can stay. Tell him he has to stay."

And then I did one of the hardest things I've ever done, I took her from Krampus and told her that another person was leaving her life forever. "He can't stay. As much as I want him to, as much as we want him to, he can't. It's not for us to decide."

"Ho! Ho! Ho! Little girls should be in bed." Standing there in front of us, out of nowhere, was Santa. The Santa.

As a kid, how I longed for this to happen. Tonight, I wanted nothing less.

Behind him stood an elf.

"Go away. You tried to steal my shoes." Thea took no prisoners.

"Ho! Ho! I don't take shoes. Filling them is the only thing that happens on my watch."

"Not you, that *thing* behind you." She was seething, and I held her tightly, almost afraid she was going to do something impulsive like try to scare him out of the house.

"I am not a thing." The elf came around Santa. "I'm Ernie the elf, and I wasn't going to *steal* them. I was just going to hide them."

"I didn't invite you into my house, and Daddy didn't, either. We are a no-elf family."

"Shhh, let's not fight with the magical people." I missed my hand being connected to Krampus's. He was going to disappear, and I couldn't do a thing about it.

"Ho! Ho! Why no elves? They make the presents I leave under the tree." Santa's belly really did wiggle. "Don't you like presents?"

"And that's another thing I'm mad about. I asked you for one thing, Santa. One thing." She started to cry, her sadness no longer masked by anger. "I was good. I even ate my vegetables. One thing."

"Why do you think I'm here?" he asked. "It's Christmas Eve, the time I deliver presents."

"You came here to take our Krampus," she sobbed. "We don't want you to take him. Tell him, Daddy. Tell him he's our Krampus and we get to keep him."

I started to open my mouth and Santa shook his head in warning, holding out his hand to Ernie and clearing his throat.

"Dear Santa, please fire Krampus. He is really bad at his job and is much better at being my Krampus Daddy. That's what I want for Christmas, and I've been good except for that sneaking-out thing, but I learned my lesson. You can count it for all the rest of my Christmas presents ever, too, so you can save a trip and shave some time off your busy night. Love, Thea." He handed it back to Ernie. "That was from you, Thea, yes?"

She nodded, sniffling.

"And you still mean it. You want Krampus to stay here with you...looking like that."

She jumped off my lap before I realized what she was doing, two firm fists on her hips. "You take it back. That was mean."

She was bossing Santa. There was no way this could end well. I stood up behind her, my hands on her shoulders. The last thing I needed was her to get close enough to kick Santa, too.

"It was mean," I said with much less vinegar than my daughter. "Krampus is the most beautiful alpha I've met since…a long time. He lights up a room just by being in it. He broke every rule there was to keep my daughter safe. Even the cat loves him. You don't need to mock his looks. You need to look at him more carefully and see the gorgeous being that he is."

"You think I'm beautiful." Krampus's hands settled on my shoulder the way mine were on Thea's. We were a family standing together in solidarity.

We were a family.

"So very." I leaned back into him. "And the thought of you leaving tonight—please don't. We'll figure out a way to keep you safe."

I turned my attention back to Santa. "What if you get him for the night he needs to…you know…and we get to keep him for the rest?"

Chapter Eighteen

Alger

He accepted me, as I was. I sat there, in Jordan's arms, lips still feeling his kiss, and listened to the things he said. He described me in ways that were totally unrelated to who I saw the last time I looked in the mirror. Beautiful? It had been a long time since that last peek at myself, but I'd have used a whole different word to relate what I viewed. Heck. There were several that applied. Ugly. Hideous. Frightening. Nightmare.

No mirror took up space in my home in the North Pole. Why would I have wanted to see anything like me looking back? And when I showered or brushed my teeth or whatever here, I just kept my gaze away from my reflection.

The description Jordan gave to Santa and Ernie...who was this person he thought he saw? For a moment, I wondered if he was under a curse, too, if Jordan had stolen a cookie from an elf by accident at some point and been cursed to think everything was the opposite of what it truly was. But, as he went on, nothing in his demeanor was anything but the regular, in-control-of-the-situation Jordan I'd come to know. As he spoke to Santa, he was looking at me.

"So you see, sir, why I entreat you to leave our Krampus here with us. My daughter and I have grown very attached to him. He is part of our family, and we love him very much." His voice was even, calm, but I'd been here long enough to recognize the passion behind the calm.

Thea, on the other hand, was anything but calm. She vibrated where she stood, but Jordan pulled her back against him, so the three of us were now connected, my hands on Jordan's shoulders, his on Thea's. Looking down at her, I saw the sparkle of a tear catch the firelight as it glistened on her cheek. "Santa, please."

The last of the ice around my heart shattered. If he didn't agree to the deal Jordan suggested, that I keep doing my job that one day of the year and live here the rest of the time, I didn't know what I'd do. I had no more of that frigid protection I'd built up the first time I was taken from my life, and I couldn't imagine being able to build it up again.

Before, I'd had a job I loved but no more, really. Not even a home to call my own. I'd been facing a lonely holiday with even my landlady, who'd pitied and been kind to me, away with her own family. In just a couple of weeks, this had become my home, and the two I held, the family I'd never dared to dream of.

"Santa, please." I echoed the little girl who held my formerly frosty heart in her little palms.

He laid a finger aside of his nose, just like in the poem, and tapped it. Santa was everything everyone believed he was. Fat and jolly and bearded, but having lived at the North Pole, I could also assert he was an excellent organizer and businessman who had chosen his husband out of love and ended up with a true partner in all things.

I had resented him not because of anything he did but because of what he did not—and could not do. For over one hundred years, I'd wanted someone to undo the curse, to give me back my life, exactly as it was. But when Thea made her request and Jordan made his suggestion, I suddenly realized that my old life not only was past and unable to be retrieved, I didn't want it. I wanted this life, the one that had begun based on a glitch in Christmas Magic.

Or was it a glitch?

Twinkling eyes met mine, and a twitch at the side of the old saint's lips told me maybe it was not. He might not have been able to undo the curse, but he had a lot of power. Of that I was sure. "Krampus, do you swear you will continue to do your duty on St. Nicholas Eve each year if I approve your change of residence?"

"Change of...yes! I do so swear." I might not have taken on the responsibilities willingly way back when, but now? "I promise."

"Then so shall it be. This Krampus will live here or wherever his family dwells going forward, and will be subject to Christmas Magic on his one night of work a year." He slapped his hands together while Ernie made notes on a tablet that had appeared out of nowhere. "Now, if a certain little lady makes herself scarce, I can do my duty and get on with my route. Thea, this year you managed to celebrate both St. Nicholas and Santa."

Her demeanor had changed when Santa said I could live with them, but the little scamp was trying her hardest to look serious now. "Yes, Santa. Double presents..."

"Right. But next year, you have to choose. Either put your shoes out for St. Nicholas or hang your stocking for Santa. Not both, understood?"

She bobbed her head.

“To bed!” he ordered, and she disappeared up the stairs in a flash, her usual stomps missing as she nearly flew. “She’ll be asleep the minute her head hits the pillow,” he told us and, after tipping his head and listening, he began to pull toys out of his pack. “I’m behind already,” he grumbled. “Goodbye, Krampus. It won’t be the same at the North Pole without you. I’m going to have to tell Mr. Claus that he won’t be getting any more of the bounty from your fishing expeditions.” His smooth brow clouded. “Not looking forward to that.”

“Perhaps,” I ventured, finally speaking up for myself, “I could come up once or twice a year and do a little fishing.” Before he could reply, I added, “It will be a good family vacation.”

“Make a note, Ernie.” The jolly old saint resumed his full persona. “Ho! Ho! Ho! Merry Christmas to all!” And the two disappeared up the chimney.

“And to all a good night,” Jordan said, turning in my arms. “I know how to make it a very good night.”

But first, despite Santa’s surety that Thea was asleep, we tiptoed up the stairs to check on her. She lay like an angel with the cat and both dogs curled up on her bed. Unusual, but that meant we’d have more privacy to have this "very good night." We tiptoed out again after tucking the covers around the little girl's shoulders.

Downstairs again, and alone, finally, we dropped to the sofa and let out a collective sigh that made the flames flicker even behind the woodstove glass window. "Am I really still here?" I felt my arm as if it might have left without me.

"I think so. Want me to pinch you to be sure?"

"I don't think so. Why would I want that?" I studied his face. "Unless that's something you like to do."

He grinned. "It's an expression. 'Somebody pinch me. I must be dreaming.' Something like that."

"It's been a long time since I've been around people except naughty children."

Jordan linked our fingers together and squeezed my hand. "Maybe it wasn't even an expression before you were cursed. I really need to hear more about how that happened, by the way. And about what you spent the last century doing."

"Tonight?" I brought our joined hands to my lips and kissed his fingers. "Because it's not a very happy story for Christmas, other than it led to me ending up here with you and Thea. I'd rather celebrate this most extraordinary night. Did you really mean you find me beautiful?" My cheeks burned. "You probably got overexcited, were being kind, defending me like Thea."

Jordan reached up and stroked my cheek. "No, not being kind. Being honest. And so was she. I don't think you've been aware of it, but you've changed a lot since you came here. But even if you hadn't, you'd be beautiful to us because we know you for who you truly are."

"Do you think I'm ordinary enough to go out in public? I mean, I don't want to model swimsuits, but just to be around people without scaring them?"

"I think you're going to have to try hard to scare them when it's your day to do that." He nestled close, burying his face in my throat.

"I think, I'm guessing Christmas Magic will help me with that." I bent and kissed him then, lips melding together, teeth and tongues engaging as our passions rose until I stood with him in my arms and started up the stairs. "I hope this is what you intended for a very good night."

"Mmm." He nibbled at my earlobe. "It's a start."

When we reached his bedroom—a room I hoped would be ours from now on because I couldn't imagine sleeping without him in my arms—I let him slide to the floor, his body grazing mine all the way down. Kisses became caresses and led to the removal of his holiday pajamas and mine. That's right, I'd been prepared to return to the North Pole in a set of flannel pajama pants Thea had picked out for me online. They were imprinted with penguins sitting on top of fluffy marshmallows and the accompanying T-shirt held the phrase, Welcome, Santa. When that little girl mounted a campaign, she did it right. Jordan's pj's were similar but with a polar bear sliding down a snowy mountainside on a peppermint disc and the phrase, Family holidays are the best, on his shirt. Santa would have had to have a heart of stone to refuse her.

But the pajamas were on the floor, the door was locked, and I was guiding Jordan to the bed when he dug his heels in. "Wait."

"I don't want to wait." My unfrozen heart was pounding a mile a minute and my cock had awoken from its long winter's nap. "Is something wrong?"

"Not wrong. But what you said before. Do you really think you look the same as when you got here? I mean, if you did, I'd still want you, but..." He took my hand and led me to the en suite where he flipped on the light. "Look in the mirror."

"What? No. I never do that." I squeezed my eyes shut. If I had to look upon my terrifying mien and misshapen form, I'd never be able to summon the nerve to make love to Jordan. I'd be far too aware of him looking at me and seeing the horror.

"Krampus...by the way, is that your name? It can't be."

"Alger, used to be my name."

"Alger, trust me and look in the mirror. I promise it's going to be good news." He held my shoulders firm and gave me a little shake. "Open your eyes."

I did because he asked me to. Because he'd never actually asked me to do anything before. Because I loved him. "W-who is that?" It had to be a painting or a photograph, but the image moved. And Jordan, my beloved Jordan was holding the man's shoulders. "It can't be me."

"It's you. I promise."

The man in the mirror's eyes filled with tears that spilled down his smooth cheeks to drop from his scruffed chin to the sink below. "I-I need a shave."

"Don't you dare shave that sexy scruff." Jordan's laughter rolled over us both until I joined him. "Now do you see what I see?"

I studied the man whose tears had turned into a flood. He was taller than Jordan but not as tall as Krampus had been which was interesting. I'd always been of greater height than most, so this was probably about right. And hair. Regular ordinary hair that could use cutting topped my head.

He wasn't handsome, but he wasn't ugly. Straight arms and legs, a flat belly, lightly furred chest, and a fully erect cock jutting out toward the mirror. "I'm ordinary."

"You're extraordinary." He grabbed my hand again. "Now, are you going to take me to bed and make some Christmas Magic, or am I going to have to beg?"

"What would that begging look like?" Visions of this handsome omega on his knees filled my mind. But I let him lead me back to the bedroom because I had to be inside him as soon as possible or embarrass myself. "I don't know how long I can last." I pressed him into the mattress, kissing every inch of his body I could get to.

He gasped when I brushed my lips over the tip of his dick. "It's been a while for me, too."

I reared back and looked at him, and he chuckled. "But not a century. I get it. It has been a century, right?"

"The elves didn't find me sexy, even if I had fallen for one of them," I assured him. "So yes, a long time."

"Then come here and let's end both our drought."

I kissed him on the lips again, sliding a finger between his bottom cheeks to find him slick and ready, so ready, for me. Poised to enter him, I hesitated just long enough for him to groan and rock his hips. "Alger...please!"

I drove inside, just the tip, wanting to go slow so as not to hurt him, but he pulled his legs back to his chest, and I took him up on the offer and plunged deep into his welcoming body. I'd been no virgin when I was human before, but it had never been like this. He was made for me, tight and hot, fitting like a glove as I plumbed his depths and retreated over and over again, longer than I'd expected but not nearly long enough.

My balls tightened, warning me, and I closed my fist around his cock and stroked in rhythm with my fucking, bringing him with me so we came together, him spraying jouts of creamy cum over his chest and mine—and me filling his body with mine.

I was ready to pull out when I swelled, knotting inside him. "This never...it's the first time," I gasped, bracing myself on my forearms. "Jordan, you're ohhh."

"You, too, Alger. It's so good."

We stayed like that until finally the knot went down then I fell to the side and brought him against me, spooned. He reached for the quilt folded at the bottom of the bed and brought it up and over us. And so we slept until Christmas morning. The best Christmas Eve leading to the best Christmas day ever.

Chapter Nineteen

Jordan

"Wake-up! Wake-up!" Thea was at the foot of my bed jumping up and down. "I wanna see my—" her hand went to her mouth as she saw Krampus by my side. Only he wasn't a Krampus anymore. He was a human. A gorgeous human with caring eyes, bed head, and the blankets up to his neck.

"You're you!" She squealed. "Like you-you, not Krampus you! When did Santa do that?"

"You know who this is?" I sat up. "How did you know?"

"Daddy, of course I know." She rolled her eyes. "Look at him. He's the same, just not and besides." She reached out and handed me a small box. "Santa left this under the tree."

I took the small box and on it was printed: *To Alger AKA Krampus.*

"That means he had to be two in one, like a superhero only Krampus style." She grabbed it from me and handed it to Alger. "Open it. I want to see what it is and then maybe we can pick out a new name for you. Alger is old, Krampus might be weird in public. Maybe Papa? I don't know. I need to think on it."

"Good morning, Thea," my love, my heart, my Krampus said. "You don't mind that I'm not the same?"

"Are you the same inside?"

He nodded.

"Do you still love Daddy?"

Another nod.

"Do you still love me?"

And a third.

"Then why would I mind? Now, open it already."

Alger tore the paper and opened the lid. Inside was a molasses cookie. "This isn't from Santa. This is from Ernie." He picked it up and looked underneath. "Look." Under the cookie sat identification. "It has my name but the wrong birthday. It's like I can start over again."

"Your last name is Bobell?" I asked, the name sounding familiar even though I couldn't quite place it.

"It was, I guess still is. I used to be a school teacher, too, can you believe? But things changed when I gave a student a cookie...Ernie's cookie."

Noel started to yip. He wanted to be up and most likely let outside.

"We shall talk about all of this and everything during breakfast. Everyone has ten minutes to get ready," I announced. "The timer starts now."

Thea ran off.

"Sorry. I—I can tell her not to just barge in our bedroom." I kissed Alger's cheek, and Noelle added her yips to the mix. "I need to let them out," I apologized.

"I'm just...this really happened. I'm me again." Eyes welled in his eyes. We'd already talked about this last night, of course, but it was probably going to take some getting used to.

"You were always you. Only difference is now you can come to the coffee shop with me and not worry about your safety." If he had stayed as he was, I'd have loved him all the same, but knowing he didn't have to stay trapped in the house was everything. "Thea's going to hold us accountable to the ten-minute breakfast start, and she's going to want all of the details."

"I'll hurry. Do you maybe have some clothing I could wear?"

"Oh yeah. Anything in the drawers, even though it might be short. I didn't think of that. I guess we will need to hit up some day-after Christmas sales."

Noel pushed into my legs. "Sorry. I either need to take care of them or clean a floor."

I grabbed some pj's and threw them on and bolted to the door to let them out. It wasn't until I let them back in that I saw our table. It was decked out in Christmas dishes and a brunch feast was laid out. On each plate was another molasses cookie. I ran to the bathroom to take care of morning business and, when I got back downstairs, Alger and Thea were at the table, nibbling on a cookie.

"Daddy! Daddy! Guess what?"

"Someone made us breakfast?" I guessed, taking my seat.

"Ernie. Ernie made us breakfast, and I'm still mad at him, but he did bring us Papa." She tasted the word. I liked it and, from the glow on Alger's face, he did, too.

"That he did." I poured a cup of what I assumed would be coffee and ended up being hot cocoa. But then again, of course it was. It was from an elf.

"But that's not the cool part. Ernie changed Papa into an elf when Papa gave Great-Great a cookie. Remember how Dad used to tell us that Great-Great hated elves because he stole his teacher—Papa was his teacher. Ernie didn't steal him...he brought him to us!" It took me a few to process all that she'd deducted.

My late husband's family had been terrified of elves in a way adults shouldn't be. And there was a story about an elf kidnapping a teacher, but it couldn't be.

"Timothy Jenkins was your great-great?" Alger asked.

"She's right? Every generation on my late mate's side of the family had a Timothy. My husband was nicknamed Theo which is how we got Thea, but...you're the kidnapped teacher?" Krampus shrugged. I had a feeling I would always think of him that way.

"Ernie knew. He always knew," Alger said more to himself than us. "So many things make sense now."

"But you know what doesn't make sense?" Thea interrupted. "Why aren't we eating? Even though I offered to trade all my presents ever for Papa, Santa still says I get gifts, and there is a huge one under the tree I want to open."

"I mean, if we have to eat the yummy food, Papa, we have to, right?" I said.

He took my hand in his at my use of his new father name. He was ours in all ways. Except on St. Nicholas Day Eve, when he was back to his task.

We ate our fill of cinnamon rolls, bacon, cookies, and all kinds of decadent delights. Thea rushed through hers, itching to get to the gifts. I couldn't blame her. It was Christmas after all.

"I guess we should wash all the dishes so we can get to the gifts." Alger stood up, plate in hand. "There are a lot here, so it probably will only take a few hours," he teased Thea, giving her a mischievous wink.

"Or we can open presents now in case Daddy got that special cleaning brush he wants," she countered, already taking her plate—just in case her plan failed.

"You asked for a cleaning brush?" Alger looked at me with an amused expression. "What a waste of a Santa request."

"It spins," I justified my wish. "Besides, no one told me I could ask for my very own Krampus. I'd have asked for that for sure."

"And this is why you both need me." Thea grabbed Trudy from the seat beside her; her doll had needed her own bacon, as usual. "Let's go already."

"Present time?" Alger asked.

"Present time."

The large gift for Thea was a house for Trudy. It took a lot for us to get it into her room, but she was completely enamored with it. Santa had gone all out.

He'd also given me the spinning dish brush and spoiled Alger with human clothes and shoes, as well as a copy of *The Night Before Christmas*. Even the pets had gifts.

"Santa outdid himself this year." I snuggled into Alger's side, the chaos of Christmas morning settling into a lazy Christmas afternoon. "But this year was brought to us by Ernie."

"I was mad at him for so many decades. Even when he was sort of my friend, I held onto it, and the entire time he was bringing me here to you." He kissed my cheek. "He brought me to my family. I love you, Jordan."

"As I love you, Krampus. As I love you." I kissed him, pouring all of my love into the kiss. This might be our first Christmas together, but it wouldn't be our last. He might've been wrong generations ago, but he was put on the earth for me. It just took some Christmas magic to get him here.

Chapter Twenty

Alger

Turned out, firewood was a really good business in a town like this. Not just the local people but all those who came to camp over the summer. With hundreds of square miles of unspoiled wilderness, lakes and valleys and trees of all kinds, our area drew tourists from all over the continental US and beyond.

The mailman had commented on our firewood pile one day, asked where we bought it, and Thea told him I had collected it all in one night. He laughed, and didn't believe the timing, but apparently he believed in my skill because he mentioned my name to a certain local businessman who showed up one day at our house to talk to me about a job.

So now, every morning I showed up at the local "Firewood for Sale" location and spent the day trekking through the forest, working on a contract with the state to thin out some of the dead trees and downed wood. We helped lower the likelihood of wildfire and made a good living for Ken and his employees at the same time. It felt good. I would never win a beauty contest, but I had improved drastically since Jordan and Thea came into my life. A sentimental person might say that their ability to see what lay behind the mien allowed it to fade? Allowed me to become more like everyone else and like I had been before the curse?

Or maybe it was this incredible area.

Or Christmas Magic.

But who wouldn't want to live here? I loved it. And, to my great surprise, I loved cutting wood for a living. My credentials as a teacher in the 1920s would not have held up in the modern world, even if I was using the name I'd had back then. What I'd taught to those children was far more basic. The three Rs. The requirements for my job were what amounted to an eighth-grade education and passing a "teacher test." Which I had with flying colors. And while I'd done a lot of reading back at the North Pole on the cold dark winter nights, I certainly didn't have the qualifications of a K-8 teacher at Thea's school. Jordan had suggested I start an online college program to teach again one day, and I might, but for now, I really enjoyed my work.

But I'd also enjoyed volunteering at the local hospital back in the day. Helping out for no money. What they now called "giving back." A way to fill in necessities and extras that paid personnel couldn't cover. At first, I'd been very shy about appearing in public, going to work and home and no place else, but one day, Jordan had a stomach bug and asked me to take Thea to school. I hated leaving him, but he seemed to be doing better after a cup of tea and some dry toast.

I'll admit I was nervous. He'd taught me to drive a modern car, and my ID from Santa included a driver's license so I was legal, but the last thing I wanted was to embarrass Thea. The drop-off line, something I'd only experienced from the passenger seat so far, seemed confusing, and if you goofed, the teacher in charge for the day could be harsh. It was also hard to let go of the whole century of being fearsome and remember that I looked pretty much like anyone else now.

Still, Jordan pointed out all I had to do was pull up in the drop-off lane and let her get out. It wasn't as complicated as I was making it, and I actually was congratulating myself on navigating it when I realized I'd made one big mistake.

She left her lunch on the seat of the car. And I should have caught that. Jordan would have for sure.

I noticed it when I stopped at the stop sign on the next corner and happened to glance into the back seat. If I carried it inside, Thea might be embarrassed at her mistake. But if I did not, Thea would be hungry. I could not let the little girl who had been mostly responsible for my entire life improvement, go all day without the sandwich she and I had made together this morning. I parked the car, took the insulated bag, and headed back toward the school.

Any hope I might have had about handing off the lunch to someone at the office was dashed when the secretary checked to see if I was on the list for Thea, found that I was, and gave me directions to her classroom. She made a joke about how in a big city it wouldn't have worked this way, and wasn't it much friendlier here?

Since I hadn't been in a school building for a hundred years...I had no idea. When I arrived at the door to Thea's class, two women were standing outside speaking in low voices, so I waited for their conversation to be over.

The older of the two, a gray-haired lady wearing a dress even I knew was at least two decades out of fashion was speaking. "Mrs. Edridge, it's your day to be class mom. You signed up for this, and we counted on your help. Are you sure you can't stay for an hour or two?"

The other, a woman around thirty who wore exercise attire shook her head. "No, I'm afraid not. Don't our taxes cover enough staffing for this school, Mrs. Buttons? It's your job to teach the children, isn't it?"

"Usually, the children and I are fine, but you know we ask each of the moms and dads to sign up for one day in the school year to help out with special projects. Today is our big spring mural painting day. Every class will be making one to hang in the auditorium for the program to be held next week. You signed up the first week of school, and I'm asking you to honor your commitment."

But the mom, whose child I pitied if she couldn't even help out one day at school, would not be convinced, and soon left, already on her phone, letting the person she was meeting for coffee know she was going to be a little late.

"Can I help you, sir?"

"I'm just dropping off Thea's lunch. I'm sorry. I didn't mean to listen in to your conversation."

She peeked into the open doorway, giving an eagle eye to the restless kids that settled them right down. I remembered doing that... "It's all right. Mrs. Edridge had a prior appointment. I just don't know how I'm going to be able to get the project done on my own though. The kids are very good, but it's an awful lot of paint..."

Making a snap decision, I pulled out my new phone. "If you need an extra set of hands, can they be mine? I'm on Thea's list." Although when I got there, I had no idea. "And her father can't make it, or I'm sure he'd want to help."

"Oh, you must be Alger. Yes, we do allow the significant others of the parents to fill in if they are signed up. You're a real lifesaver. Are you sure you have the time?" She stood at least two inches taller in her relief.

"Well I need to check with my boss, but I'm sure he'll say yes." Hopefully. Because if he said no, I was going to need a new job.

Not having mastered texting yet, I called my boss. He said yes. It didn't hurt that his son Ozzie was in Thea's class. He gave me the whole day off. With pay. And promised to charge Mrs. Edridge double for her wood next winter.

Being back in the classroom had my mood soaring. By the time I left at noon and headed for home, I couldn't wait to tell Jordan all about my day. The kids had been really nice, and we'd created a work of art for the spring program.

I was even invited to attend!

I'd sent a text to Jordan a bit earlier, and he'd assured me he was fine and I didn't need to rush, but I was glad to be getting home at noon instead of my usual late-afternoon time. I could see for myself he was okay and then pop back for Thea when she got out of class. Having mastered drop-off, I felt confident I could handle pickup. I made a quick swing past the Dinerette for a bowl of their famous chicken soup on Thea's teacher's recommendation and arrived home to find Jordan sitting in the living room bundled in a blanket.

It was a cool spring day, so the blanket didn't worry me, but his pale cheeks did.

"Jordan, you said you were fine. You don't look fine at all."

He gave me a wan smile. "There's nothing wrong that won't be all better in about eight months."

"What?" I set the bag with the soup on the counter and flew to his side, dropping onto my knees beside him. "You've already seen a doctor, then? And he said you're going to be sick that long? This is unacceptable. We'll go to a specialist." Even in my day, people did that. "We'll find someone in the city who can resolve this in a whole lot less time than that."

He stroked my hair and stopped me from patting his arms and legs, as if I might find something there to explain his long-term mystery illness. "If you'd just stop, I'll explain." He held out a plastic stick. "Look at this."

"I don't know what that is." I brushed it aside. "We need to get you taken care of as quickly as possible."

"Alger, it's going to take eight months to finish growing this baby." He waved the stick at me. "This is a pregnancy test. I peed on the stick, and it shows that I am pregnant. We're going to have a baby."

Okay, I might have blacked out for a minute, but when I woke up, I looked at Jordan's concerned expression hovering over me and reached up to enfold him in my arms. "I never dreamed I'd be a father. When I was cursed, I just assumed..."

"Is this okay? You don't mind?"

"Mind?" I kissed him over and over, covering his face with a thousand kisses. "Is it a boy or a girl?" I reached for the stick to see if it would tell me, but he laughed and waved my hand away.

"I really did pee on this, so you probably don't need to touch it. Anyway, it's too soon to know anything more than that it's a baby on the way."

We went together to pick up Thea. We couldn't wait any longer to tell her, and of course she was as thrilled as we were. We probably didn't even need to butter her up with the hot fudge sundae.

Chapter Twenty-One

Jordan

"When are you getting married?" Thea asked and I nearly choked on my shepherd's pie.

"Thea," I said in warning. It wasn't that I didn't want to marry Alger. I did. But we hadn't discussed that at all yet, and doing so by means of a dinner blurting was less than ideal.

"Daddy." She met my eyes.

"That is for grown-ups to discuss, not little girls."

"Ernie's an elf, not a grown-up, and I heard him talking with Papa about it. Why can Ernie talk about it and not me? He's not even part of our family," she countered. I feel bad for anyone she has to debate when they start doing those in class. She's gonna cream them.

"Ernie was here?" I didn't hate Ernie.

My feelings for him were complicated. He scared my late husband's family for generations, and that sucked. It also sucked that the kids thought their teacher quit mid-year, for that was the story Timothy had been told when he shared what happened with his grown-ups at the time. But then again, he did all of that to bring our family together in the here and now. Regardless, he couldn't keep bebopping in and out of our house. That was just plain rude.

"I called him," Alger said. "I wanted to ask him a favor."

"Oh." I turned my attention right back to Thea. "It's rude to eavesdrop, and it often results in you misunderstanding things and feeling bad about them. It's never a good plan."

She pouted and opened her mouth to contradict me. I stopped her with my *Dad Eyes* as she called them.

"Now let's get back to this delicious meal." Alger had made it using a recipe from the school cookbook he helped organize as a fundraiser. It was great seeing him so active at the school. I imagined he'd be there as a teacher before long. Most of his education really didn't fit what teachers needed now, but he was picking up on everything quickly and doing exceedingly well in his current classes.

"I asked Ernie to stop by for a favor," Alger said again.

"Was he able to help you?" I set my fork down, giving him all my attention. I hadn't meant to cut him off. I thought he'd just been making a comment.

"He was." Alger got up and went over to the counter, grabbing our cookie jar, the one we picked up at a secondhand store. It had a picture of a Krampus on it, walking through the woods with their basket on their back. The store called it creepy and gave it to us for a buck.

Alger set it on the table and opened it up. "This was in my family but got lost in the whole me-becoming-a-Krampus thing."

He took a cookie out and set it on his plate.

"Not that," he chuckled, grabbing another cookie. This time it went to Thea. A third cookie to me, two dog bone cookies for Noel and Noelle, and a ball with a bell in the middle later, and he was standing there holding a small wooden box. "I guess Ernie wanted something for everyone."

He opened the small box and held it out to me. Inside were two identical rings. "They belonged to my parents. My alpha father wore his before it was in vogue. He wanted my omega father to know that he was honored to be his husband. They passed when I was barely a man, and I kept these for my one-day husband."

Thea jumped out of her chair and raced over to Alger, throwing her arms around him. "Now you will for real be my papa. You won't have to be the 'significant other' like they say at school when you come in. You will be mine for real."

He set the ring box down and hugged her. "I am for real even if your father doesn't want to get married. We're family. You're stuck with me." I adored the way he reassured her so, pushing aside the nerves he had to be feeling. Asking someone to marry you was kind of a big deal.

But then again, we'd already gone through the *begging Santa to let him stay* thing. This might be far less intense than if we met and dated the normal way.

"But he will say yes." I went to them, hugging them both. "Of course I'll say yes. I love you, Alger."

"Yes!" She fist-bumped because of course she did. "Now, let's get back to dinner." She was so matter-of-fact all of a sudden.

"Yeah, okay." We broke our hug and, as she scurried back to her seat, I snuck in a kiss.

"I love you so much, my beautiful Krampus. Of course I want to be yours for always."

"Dinner," Thea said curtly, and we both obeyed, just shaking our heads.

“This is really good,” I agreed, scooping up a large forkful.

“It’s fine. I just need to finish it so I can get to Ernie’s cookie. Do you think he’s going to come to the wedding?” she asked, her mouth full. She was determined to get to that cookie. And really, I didn’t blame her. The elf knew how to bake.

“We don’t even know when we’re getting married yet. There’s still a lot to discuss.” I reached out my hand for Alger. “But we promise to let you know when we know.”

My first wedding had been planned for us by my late husband’s family. It had been traditional and fine. But Alger and I had a relationship that was far from traditional. I had a feeling the same would be true for our wedding.

“Or you could let me help. I’m really good at planning tea parties. Trudy and I had one this morning and she said it was the best she had ever been to.” Of course, Trudy was a doll, and the tea party consisted of empty plastic plates and teacups.

“I mean, if Trudy said it’s the best.” Alger looked straight at Trudy who was at her own seat at the table. “So we should let her help, Trudy?”

"Yes," Thea said in her *doll* voice.

"Then that settles it. We shall plan this as a family." Alger squeezed my hand.

"As a family," I agreed.

I loved the sound of that.

Chapter Twenty-Two

Alger

With a wedding planner like Thea, it was a wonder we didn't have two hundred dozen roses and enough balloons to lift the house off its foundations. She was so excited from the moment we told her we were getting married and she was going to be part of the ceremony.

In the months since first Jordan and Thea and then I had moved to this community, we'd built some relationships with people we saw all the time, but this ceremony and the reception afterward would be attended by not only them but by the family and friends who had tried to help them after Thea's dad died. All the people who had hosted them for the holidays and tried very hard to remind them that life went on.

If they had not done that, I don't know what would have become of them. My gratitude knew no bounds, and I wanted to do the very best I could to show my appreciation. Our guests filled the local motel, the bed-and-breakfast, and the guest rooms at several friends' homes. It was going to be the event of the summer, and if we hadn't had such a nice big yard, we'd have had to rent the school auditorium to fit them all in.

But as it was, we covered the mountains of firewood still under the porch with tarps and then canvas in our colors of sage and Venetian red. Not traditional, but we loved them. And in the summery outdoors, they made sense. We'd commissioned a local artist to paint that canvas with our names and the date, and it looked festive and not like a way to hide a wood pile. Tables and chairs were scattered around the yard, outdoor furniture borrowed from friends and some from the school as well. The tables were all covered in the cloths we'd ordered in our colors, so they looked somewhat uniform, except for the shapes, but the chairs were all different, which I thought gave the whole thing a charming rusticity.

Back in my day, there were no rental places for events such as this, and while we had a good income between us, we'd decided not to waste money on things we didn't need to and to save them for things we loved, like the gorgeous centerpieces of greenery and a really unique lily in exactly the right red. And our tuxes.

I'm afraid I'd become something of a clothes horse after having to make do for so long in the Krampus outfit of leggings and cloak or the generic outerwear Santa had managed to stock that would actually fit over my giant, twisted form. Still not a model, I had a body that could be clothed in a suit, and Jordan... Well, my Jordan, in my humble opinion, should be on the cover of a magazine in the tux he was currently walking down the aisle in. We didn't have any wedding attendants other than his cousin standing up for him and my boss for me.

And of course Thea.

Who was the star of the show. Instead of a frou-frou dress, she'd decided to wear a tux like her "two daddies." Everyone clapped when she preceded Jordan down the aisle. Even me. But Jordan...the sight of him made my heart pound in my ears. Not just because he was so handsome, although he was, but because he was Jordan. Jordan of the kind eyes, Jordan who had welcomed me into his home—and his bed. Jordan who told Santa Claus I was beautiful.

My Jordan.

He reached the front row of folding chairs from the school auditorium and I moved closer to take his hand. Thea's teacher, Mrs. Buttons, had signed up to be a wedding celebrant at some online site just to be part of our big day, and she stood there in her flowered dress, a hat with a tiny veil and bunch of cherries on the side perched on her gray-haired head, beaming at us. "Welcome everyone to Alger and Jordan's wedding. I know some of you have come from quite far away, and they've asked me to thank you and ask that you all join together in a short prayer for their future life together..." The prayer was her idea, but since Christmas Magic brought us together, it seemed like a very good idea.

The ceremony flew by after that, and it seemed only seconds before we were kissing each other then scooping up Thea and both kissing her on the cheek at the same time. Bless the photographer who caught that shot because it was going on the wall as soon as I could get it printed out.

The sun shone down on us all day, with only a few puffy white clouds to decorate the sky, and when the sun set, the dancing began. Local musicians had volunteered their services which we gratefully accepted, and I spent the first evening of my marriage with my new husband in my arms, twirling around under a full golden moon. We'd been told to have an alternative plan in case of rain, but Jordan refused to believe the magic would let us down at this point and, very fortunately, he was right.

Thea flaked out sometime around ten, and Ken and his husband, who had offered to babysit so we could spend a few days alone together, left with her piled in the back seat of their SUV with their own kids.

Gradually everyone else left, too, until it was only us and the mess in our yard. I looked around in dismay. “We can’t go to bed and leave it like this.”

Jordan smiled at me. “The food is all put away and anything else a bear might want to go through is safely in the trash. The rest can wait until morning, unless you’d like to spend our wedding night folding up chairs and tables.”

“You look extra handsome in the moonlight, husband.” I held out my arms, and he stepped into them. “So, no, I think I’d rather take you inside and show you how much I love you.”

“I think that’s a good plan.” We turned and together began to climb the stairs to the porch. “We could also hunt down more firewood.” He laughed. “But we might have enough.”

"If not, I'll find you as much as you want." I brushed my lips on the top of his head. "After I bend you over the couch and..."

His breathing harshened. "The couch. Not the bed?"

"With a certain person out of the house, I thought we might take a tour of the various rooms of the house and see how much mischief we can get into in them." I winked. "If you're game."

"I'm game, but you know what happens to the mischievous." His voice lowered. "A Krampus comes for them."

I lifted him in my arms and took the steps two at a time. "Only if they're very lucky."

Chapter Twenty-Three

Jordan

"You were supposed to be here yesterday." I held my belly, giving our baby a stern talking to. "And since you weren't, you need to wait until tomorrow."

It was just before December 5th, the one day of the entire year that my husband couldn't be here for the birth of our child. He was already gone, December 5th coming earlier in some parts of the world than ours.

My belly tightened again. This was not good. This was very not good.

"Daddy, who you talking to? Is Cookie with you?" Thea's voice came through the bathroom door. "Is Papa home early?"

"No, sweet girl, he's not." I opened the door. "I was talking to your new brother or sister."

"They being naughty already?" She let out a long sigh. "Papa told them to be good and stay put until he got home. They should be good. Tonight is not the night to mess with Papa."

"It's the night you met him, and how did that turn out?" I reminded her. "He saved you and made our family whole."

"That was different. I wasn't naughty."

I gave her my *dad look*. "I was trying to be helpful, and besides, he's not even scary. Anyone who meets him knows that."

"So then it's fine for your sibling to 'mess with Papa.'"

She just rolled her eyes.

"Let's go watch a Christmas movie." I pointed out the door for her to leave. I was huge. The two of us could not come close to squeezing through the door together, not with my baby bump the size of a small county.

"Do I get to pick? I heard there was a new movie about Papa." She skipped out of the room.

"It's not new, and no. We will never watch that one." Ever. "It's a horror movie and not about Papa. It just has his name."

I waddled out behind her and down the stairs. If things were progressing the way they had been, I had a full two minutes to get to the couch. I was crossing my fingers for longer. I didn't want to have this baby without Alger. But I refused to break our agreement and lose him forever over my own insecurities over having a baby alone.

I refused.

"I'm gonna make popcorn," she said more than asked, and I let her. It was one of the new things she had in her "cooking" repertoire. It was only the microwave kind, not the good stuff, but it made her happy and would hopefully distract her if another contraction came through.

Which it did. This one worse than the one before. I was going to have to cave and call the midwife soon. But doing that made it real, and it wasn't allowed to be real. Not until my Krampus was home from Krampus duty.

"Want some?" She came skipping back in with a bowl full.

"Not right now, but I found a movie." It was the first one on the screen when I asked for Christmas movies. That was the extent of searching I'd done. It was hard to make decisions when it felt like someone had your middle in vise grips.

"*Elf*! Ernie would love this one. I should invite him." She all but threw the bowl in my lap and bounded up the stairs to her special *Ernie* phone. He'd given it to her when they first forged their friendship. Thea forgave him for the shoe thing rather quickly when she found out it was all to help her keep her Krampus. The phone was a toy to anyone else, but for us it rang the North Pole.

Most kids get a cell phone for their first phone. My kid? She got a direct line to Santa and his elves.

I went to stop her, my contraction deciding that wasn't going to happen, the popcorn spilling on the floor as I tried to hold in my cry. Tried and failed. She came tumbling down the stairs, phone in hand.

"Daddy, what happened?" She rushed to me, the popcorn crushing beneath her feet.

"Nothing. Your sibling is just thinking it's time to show up." I was out of breath, but my words were clear. That was something. Had she arrived less than a minute earlier, I'd have probably screamed instead of using words.

"You're having a baby...now...when Papa is working?" Her eyes went wide. "What do we do?"

"We do nothing. It takes a long time for babies to come and, if Papa comes home early, we break our promise."

She gave a nod of understanding.

"Maybe you can be a big girl and clean this up. I don't think I can."

"Sure." She brought the phone to her ear. "I gotta go, Ernie. Talk to you soon." She slid it into her pocket.

"Wait? Was he on the phone the entire time?"

She gave me a nod.

Please don't let him interfere. I refused to lose my husband because we can't keep our promise. I refuse.

"Let's get this cleaned up." I wasn't going to bite off trouble I couldn't chew, not when I had a baby to try and convince to stay put.

"I'll be back, Daddy." She held the bowl of popcorn she'd cleaned up off the floor. "Don't have my sister without me."

"We talked about this. It might be a brother," I reminded her.

"It's my sister and we're going to name her Cindy Lou." She jogged out.

"I won't let that happen to you, little one." I closed my eyes, the feeling of another contraction already stirring. The odds of me having this baby without Alger were high.

"What's the story?" Ernie was suddenly in front of me. Great.

"It's fine, Ernie," I lied, teeth clenched as I tried my best to school my face.

"If by fine you mean you're in active labor, then yes it is."

I didn't answer him, the pain getting to be too much. But I was going to have words for him after this contraction. That was for sure.

"Ernie! Can you get Papa?"

"No!" It came out as more of a bellow than I'd intended, the agony too much to mask. "Promise."

"Promise what?" she asked, now at my side. "Promise what, Daddy?"

"We promised Santa." Didn't they understand?

Ernie came over and held my hand, and the next thing I knew, I was in my bed...naked. I wasn't even going to ask him how he did that. I very much didn't want to know.

He was there, then gone, then back again. "Thea is taking care of the pets. I'm going to get your husband but not until it is time."

"You can't. I'll...we'll lose him."

"Pish. I'm the king of loopholes." Unlike when Thea used it, I was pretty sure Ernie knew exactly what that word meant. "Now let's get you as close as we can without being too late."

Ernie stayed by my side, helping me remember my breathing exercises, bringing me ice chips, walking with me as I paced the room, and encouraging me the entire way. It was a long labor, crossing into our December 5th. Ernie was amazing, remembering to mind Thea and even the dogs once she fell asleep.

Midafternoon the next day, my body was wrung out. I wasn't sure I could do this anymore. That was when Ernie decided it was time to get my husband. Only he didn't tell me that was what he was up to, instead saying he'd be right back like he'd done a thousand times already.

"I'm not too late." In front of me stood Krampus, with his basket and everything. He shucked the basket and sat at my side. "Don't look at me."

"Oh, my sweet, amazing mate, you are the only one I want to see right now." I reached up and ran a finger around one of his horns and then down to his cheek. "Our baby is almost here. Hold my hand?"

Only a couple of rapid contractions later, I felt the urge to push. Ernie helped with the delivery. Alger, my Krampus, was by my side and, when the first cry filled the room, a joy I'd only ever known once before flooded through me.

"You have a baby boy." Ernie handed me our sweet baby, magically cleaned up and swaddled.

"You are so sweet," I said, looking down at him with tear-filled eyes. "Did you see your papa?"

"Don't. I'm too—"

"Papa!" Thea came barging into the room and threw her arms around him. "I forgot how good you look as Krampus. Will the baby be a Krampus, too? That would be so cool."

"The baby is your brother, and he was just born," I chided gently.

Her gaze shot straight to me, her smile growing even wider.

"The baby will not be a Krampus unless he steals my cookie," Ernie said with a laugh.

"We can't keep calling him the baby," Thea insisted, quite correctly. "We should name him Ernie. Ernie is the reason we got Papa, and without Papa, there would be no baby."

Her reasoning was sound.

"Ernie is a nickname," Alger said. "Ernest is the full name."

"I was always Ernie," the elf corrected.

"Ernie?" I looked up at my husband.

"Ernie," Alger agreed.

"This has been fun and all," Ernie said, "but I need to get you out of here so Ernie doesn't grow up to have hooves." He said it with jest, but there was urgency in his voice.

"Goodbye, my sweet boy," Alger said to our son. "I love you, Jordan. I'll be back as soon as I can." He climbed off the bed, ruffling Thea's hair on his way to Ernie. "I'm ready. You'll come back and make sure they're okay?" he asked the elf.

"Your son is my namesake. He has the protection of all the elves," he said and, off they went to do the work of Christmas Magic as I held my own Christmas Magic in my arms. I'd never even called the midwife, and I'd have to deal with her questions later because Ernie and my Krampus had done just fine without her help.

Epilogue

Alger

Christmas Day

"Are you sure he doesn't know?" Thea's stage whisper carried halfway across Santa's Village, but who could blame her? As she'd pointed out multiple times in the last half hour, how many other kids got to ride home with Santa on Christmas morning?

Well, one other kid did—her little brother, but he was less than a month old and would have to rely on her memory of events if he wanted to tell his friends. Not that he should. Or that she should. Santa had sworn Thea to secrecy about the whole thing, warning her that if she didn't "zip it up" regarding her visit to the North Pole, she'd be on the naughty list for sure. And the visit on St. Nicholas Eve wouldn't be from the Krampus she knew and loved but one of my associates.

That should do it. Because even I couldn't guarantee that they were as easygoing as me. But Thea could keep a secret as she'd proven over and over since I joined the family.

"Where do they make the marshmallows?" Jordan asked, cuddling little Ernie close. "I want to find out where we've been going wrong."

He'd become more than obsessed with the sweet treats since our attempts failed every time. "After we pay our visits, I'll take you to the shop," I promised. I was more concerned about what shape my old home was in. Likely not the best place to take a baby, but I hoped to get some help fixing it up for future trips. For this one, we had other accommodations.

Elves gathered on street corners, whispering to one another. I didn't blame them for being curious. In all my years as a Krampus, I'd never seen an outsider on the premises. Only special approval from Santa based on my promising to do some ice fishing for his Mr. Claus had gotten him to pick us up on his way back this morning.

"Cocoa!" Thea was racing toward a shop with a Santa-faced mug painted on the window, but I grabbed her arm. "I want some!"

"Thea, if Santa is good at knowing how you behave at a distance, how good do you think he is when he can actually see you," Jordan said.

We all turned around to find Santa still standing by the sleigh. He raised a mittened hand in a friendly wave, but Thea paled. "I guess he can see me good."

"Well," I corrected her. "He can see you well."

Jordan rolled his eyes. "Looks like the teacher is coming out again."

"Yes, it's been a long time, but between spending time at Thea's school and my online classes, I'm on the way. With the background Santa set up for me, I'm officially two years away from a credential. I'm even going to be able to student teach with Mrs. Buttons." The sweet elderly teacher was also a master teacher and was helping me so much.

We strolled along for a while, Thea and Jordan's heads pivoting to see each site. I feared they'd end up with whiplash by the time we got to Ernie's place. I'd never actually been to visit him there, but I did know where it was, and a block past the marshmallow shop we came to the molasses cookie store.

"Ready, Thea?" I pointed to the staircase running up the side of the building. "Your friend Ernie lives over his shop."

She bounced in her glee but then placed a finger on her lips and tiptoed up the stairs. We stood below, passing the bundled-up baby back and forth as Thea arrived at the wooden door and rapped firmly. "Delivery!" she crooned. "Delivery for Ernie the elf."

I leaned close to Jordan. "Is it me, or is she using a very deep voice?"

He chuckled. "It's not you. She's been practicing."

The door clicked open to reveal Ernie in a bathrobe with a towel wrapped around his hair. "I was in the tub. I didn't order anything, I—Thea!"

"Yes, it's me!" She grabbed his hands and bounced up and down even more than before. "And my fathers and my brother, and we're here for Christmas and to go fishing and to see all the shops and to..." Her voice trailed off as she dragged Ernie inside with her. I shrugged and started up the stairs in time to hear, "And we are staying at Santa Claus's house, and you're invited for Christmas dinner and..."

Yes, we were staying at Santa's house while we fixed up my old home. We'd be fishing and shopping and visiting because Santa promised that Krampuses were no longer going to be treated as second-class citizens. They were every bit as important as any other part of Christmas Magic, and he had apologized for not recognizing how I felt. How we felt.

I was also going to meet the others. Finally. And tell them they, too, could have a life beyond one day a year.

Just inside the door, I paused and looked up.

Jordan followed my gaze. "Mistletoe." He smiled. "Even up here, huh?"

"Especially up here. And the tradition is firm." I cupped his cheek and stared into the eyes of the man who had made my every day as special as Christmas. And then I kissed him under the mistletoe at the North Pole, savoring his lips against mine until a tug on my pant leg returned my attention to where we were. And the baby cradled between us.

She'd tugged on my pants before.

Mister, are you Santa's helper?

Now, I knew I was. In a big way.

About the Author

Lorelei M. Hart is the cowriting team of USA Today Bestselling Authors Kate Richards and Ever Coming as well as Ophelia Heart, another bestselling author. Friends for years, the trio decided to come together and write one of their favorite guilty pleasures: Mpreg. There is something that just does it for them about smexy men who love each other enough to start a family together in a world where they can do it the old-fashioned way.

Sign up for our Newsletter here**.**

Check out the Shifters of Distance
The Crimson Cliff Pack Series
Manny's Mannies
Omegas of Animals
Lorelei's Amazon Page

Made in the USA
Middletown, DE
21 February 2025